THE BOOKIE

A JACOB SCHREIBER MYSTERY

Guy Verreault

PublishAmerica
Baltimore

© 2004 by Guy Verreault.
All rights reserved. No part of this book may be reproduced, stored in a retrieval system or transmitted in any form or by any means without the prior written permission of the publishers, except by a reviewer who may quote brief passages in a review to be printed in a newspaper, magazine or journal.

First printing

This book is a work of fiction. Names, characters and incidents are either the products of the author's imagination or are used fictitiously. Any resemblance to actual events or persons, living or dead, is entirely coincidental.

ISBN: 1-4137-4162-2
PUBLISHED BY PUBLISHAMERICA, LLLP
www.publishamerica.com
Baltimore

Printed in the United States of America

Dedication

This is to the best companion a man could ever have, my wife Inge, who waited twenty-five years for me to fulfil my promise of writing a novel or two or three or more.

Acknowledgments

Thanks to:

Gwen MacPherson for her professional proofreading

My son John for his almost weekly technical advice

My sister Colette, an author of several books, who found my work "extraordinaire," but English!

David Bell, a friend with timely advice

Rolf Engelhardt, for his practical gift

FRED KADE, for letting me use him as a sounding board

Other friends, acquaintances and relatives who at times probably thought I was off my rocker. "If they only knew!"

Also in the Jacob Schreiber Mystery series:

The Piano Player

Forthcoming:

The Dog Walker

The Runaway Surgeon

The Reluctant Juror

CHAPTER ONE...

(September 1945)

    The morning sun was still peering through the smog on Hollywood Boulevard. Early morning brought two different species of society to life: the working class hurrying to get where they had to go and the leftovers from the night before. Some, too drunk to go home, had slept on the sidewalk either directly in store entrances or close to them. The smell of vomit and urine was strong where the night warriors had fallen. Six-thirty in the morning and Jacob was on his way to the office at Hollywood and Vine. Above the stench of the streets he could smell fresh brewing coffee. A good cup of coffee is all he wanted at this time of the day. He had an apartment on Sunset near Fairfax and when the weather permitted, which was 95% of the time, he preferred walking to his office. As he approached the building, he could see several police cars parked some on the sidewalk. He wondered what could have happened. Probably someone was beaten to death. A police officer recognized Jacob and told him Lieutenant Jones was inside and would like to talk to him. Now Jacob's curiosity was piqued, and he ran up the two flights of stairs to his office. The old elevator was out of order. From the landing, he could see the print on the glass door: "Jacob Schreiber, Private Investigator. Divorces, Surveillance, You name it, I do it," in bold black with a trim of deep gold. He was proud of that sign. It had brought him many clients who really did not know what a PI was in 1945. As he approached the door, he could see the silhouette of men moving around inside. He wondered what the hell was going on here!

"There you are, Jacob," was the greeting he got from Los Angeles Police Lieutenant Bill Jones. "We got a call someone had been shot in this building early this morning. When the patrol officer got here and realized this was your office, he immediately put in a call for me. Your door had been left wide open, obviously the lock had been jimmied and the body could be seen from the hallway." The lieutenant motioned Jacob to walk over to where the body was lying face down. The man had been shot in the back of the skull, blood was all over the place.

"The body was still warm when we got here, Jacob, so we figure the man was shot less than three hours ago, probably at about 4 AM. The coroner will try to confirm that." As he leaned down and turned the body over, he asked Jacob, "Do you know this guy?"

Jacob leaned forward and looked carefully at the man's shattered face. Yes, he did recognize the face but quickly debated if he should confirm that with the lieutenant.

"This is Louis 'The Snake' Billings as he was known. A bookie, loan shark, pimp, with many unmentionable undertakings only a low life individual like Louis would be involved in. His wife had hired me to tail him for divorce procedures about three months ago. He was not my client, but I did meet him face-to-face once or twice. Why would somebody kill him in my office I wonder?"

Jacob proceeded to look around. If there was anything missing, he could detect it at first glance. Then he unlocked the heavy metal filing cabinet and started to go through it, drawer by drawer. He obviously could not immediately tell if any files were missing. Anne Dombrowski, his secretary, would be in later around 10 o'clock. She would be able to tell if something was missing.

"OK, Lieutenant, I can't see what he was doing here, but someone followed Louis here and did away with him. Since the divorce proceedings were coming up shortly, I can only imagine he was looking for the file I had on him. Do you know his wife's address? I have it here if you need it. Did you want me for anything else, Lieutenant?"

"Not at this time, Jacob. Maybe in a day or two, once I have more information on this character and the autopsy report, it might enlighten me. I'm going to have the coroner remove the body. The investigators are done with the picture taking and I imagine it would be useless to dust for prints. Just keep in touch with me in case you find something unusual, and knowing you, it will probably happen that way. We have known each other for a long time, Jacob, and I want you to know I have a lot of respect for you. You play the game fair and that's the way I like it. The time you spent with the Marines in the South Pacific during the war helped build your character. My brother was your commanding officer and he talked about you a lot."

"Thanks, Lieutenant, you can always count on my cooperation. Should I find something of importance to attach to this slimy bastard, you'll be the first to know."

After the body was removed and the police had left, Jacob sat at his desk. The whole office was one room about 30 feet by 20 feet. He had a small private office space walled off with tinted glass. It did not reach the ceiling, which happened to be around 12 feet high in this old building. The window from his second floor office overlooked Hollywood Boulevard to the west. It was the only window in the office. The air conditioning was central and at times it didn't work properly, which made it stuffy for the reception area. There were only two chairs for clients to sit on, both in his office and the reception area.

He decided to call Helen Billings to hear her reaction on Louis' departure from planet Earth. After six rings, there was still no answer. He hung up, took a walk down the stairs and headed straight for the front door. There was still a commotion going on outside. The curious wanted to know from the police what was going on or what had happened. The officer, who obviously had a strong sense of humor and some dislike for him, was telling the curious ones that some crazy "gumshoe," and by that he meant Jacob, had killed himself. When the officer saw him coming out the door, Jacob thought he detected a bit of immediate redness on his face. He pretended he had not heard him and kept on walking towards Schwab's for coffee. Some of the studio crowd were regulars at the lunch counter.

When Jacob walked in, he could see there were a few "wannabe's" sipping early morning coffee, probably spiced up. The gumshoe sat at the counter and was served a hot mug of his favorite java. Jennie, the waitress, blurted out, "What's going on in your building, flatfoot? I hear some guy got bumped off right in front of your desk. Is that true?"

She stood there looking straight at him, waiting for an answer. Her question had not disturbed anyone else in the joint. This is Hollywood you know. The patrons were used to hearing actors reciting script lines aloud, so this one was no different to them. To Jacob it was. "Yes, Jennie," he said, "some poor bastard was sent to the Promised Land without a return ticket. He didn't even have a chance to speak to me about it. How do you like that? I'm glad I wasn't in the office when it happened. You know, I could be following his deadly footsteps."

She smiled, showing those big white molars, and walked away without saying a word. Death had become a mystified event in the world of dreamers aspiring to become part of the big screen. Someone being shot and killed in an office, to them, was no different from someone being shot "à la Al Capone" on the big screen in a movie theater. The private eye gulped his coffee and ordered a fresh one to go. He took a walk back to reality, his second floor office.

When he arrived at the building, all bystanders were gone. Even the police officer that had been standing guard had left. He walked up the stairs as fast as he could. Somehow Jacob had the feeling the police had overlooked something. What that something was, he couldn't tell right away, but he would give it a shot.

To his surprise, Anne had already arrived. "You're early, Miss Dombrowski," he said in an official tone. "Did you hear about the guy being snuffed out right here in the office?"

"First of all, Jacob, it's after ten. Secondly, the police officer that was standing guard outside the main entrance joyfully filled me in on the morning news. Now if you would like to inform me with more details, I'm willing to listen. Was this guy a client of ours? On the

THE BOOKIE

other hand, is it a case of wrong identity? Don't look surprised, Jacob, you know what I mean. Was it supposed to be you?"

"You know, Anne, you would have made a good prosecutor. Maybe you should go back to UCLA and pursue a law degree. Questions, questions, you fire them like a machine gun. This is what makes you so efficient in this business. No, the guy was not a client, but the husband of a client. You remember Helen Billings, she hired me to find dirt on her husband. She was going to file for divorce and just needed additional bits and pieces to blow him away. I did find some items of interest on Louis 'The Snake' Billings. I know the case was due for court shortly, but now, she won't have to go through the mudslinging. I wonder if she had him removed from the society registry. Do you think Helen Billings could have done it?" Jacob asked. "There were no signs of struggle, which usually is a telling tale the victim knew the assailant."

Anne answered, "From what I can recall of the little lady, I don't think Helen Billings is capable of committing premeditated murder. Hiring someone to do it, that's another story. I remember how small she is physically from her first visit here. Barely over five feet tall and maybe 100 pounds, kind of a shy person, not your normal description of a hitman. No, I don't think she could have done it, Jacob. Here's the file on Mrs. Billings, including the photos you took of her husband with what appears to be call girls. Have you talked to her about it yet?"

"No, Anne, I tried once and no one answered the telephone. It just kept on ringing. After six or seven rings, I hung up." As he opened the file, Jacob noticed the telephone number listed didn't look like the number he called earlier. Jacob walked to his desk and came back with Helen Billings' card. "Guess what? The last two digits are 98 and old dummy here dialed 89 as written on my card. I must have transposed the numbers in that manner when I took them from your file. I had better give her a call again. Thanks for enlightening me, as usual."

CHAPTER TWO...

    The day had really begun on the wrong foot for Jacob. He sat at his desk, just reminiscing the events of the morning. The LAPD had been all over his office, snooping at whatever they could see. His files had not been touched. Lieutenant Jones made sure of that. During his stint with the Marines in the South Pacific, Jacob's commanding officer was Octavio Jones, older brother of now police lieutenant Bill Jones. His training in San Diego and war action from mid-1942 to the end of the war had taught him discipline. He had been a model marine, tough and obedient.
    When he returned to southern California after his discharge, he moved to Hollywood. The glamour of the movie studios is not what attracted him. One of his marine buddies, who unfortunately did not return alive, had told him about a relative who had a thriving private detective agency. His friend had mentioned how easy it had been for his uncle to make fast money in a legal way. Divorces and security were the two main workloads. He thought that maybe he and Jacob could open a similar business in the Hollywood area. Demand for surveillance and security had increased two fold in the past five years, he told Jacob. The idea was one Jacob liked. His father had been killed on duty while serving as an LAPD officer on the downtown beat. When his friend was killed in the South Pacific, he pushed the dream of private investigator aside. It all came back to him while being processed for release in San Diego in late summer 1945. He had sufficient money to survive for a short time. Someone had told him about grants and interest-free loans one could get once out of the armed forces. He made inquiries and within a month was enrolled in a criminal investigation course organized by the Los Angeles county sheriff department for new recruits and people with an interest in the criminal justice system. He graduated with honors, top of his class. He could have joined the Sheriff's department but

THE BOOKIE

declined. At 6'3", 205 pounds he was in great physical condition. Jacob's top marks and positive attitude did not go unnoticed by other law enforcement agencies. The FBI, the Highway Patrol and the LAPD all tried to recruit him. He declined them all. Jacob wanted to test his dream of having his own business as a private investigator.

He found this hole in the wall office space in an older building near Hollywood and Vine. This area was perfectly suited for a Private Eye's office. A hub of activities, it had all the necessary elements to draw business. His beginnings had been modest. Through friends from the war days, he made some good contacts that brought business his way. These were his thoughts when continuous knocking on his office door took him out of his rêverie.

"Jacob, there's someone here to see you," Anne said. "Do you want me to bring her in now? It's a Lucy Meyer; she says she has some information which could be important to you. She said to me she hated the cops because they roughed her up one time when she had been drinking."

"Bring the lady right in, Anne," said a smiling PI.

"I don't know why I'm here," said a nervous Lucy Meyer.

"Take your time, Mrs. Meyer," Jacob said

"It's Miss Meyer, never been married, never intend to do so. I've seen too many marriages go down the drain lately. I don't know why these women are in such a rush, Mr. Schreiber. They make it look as if it's the last thing they're going to do in their lives. Then 'bang,' six months, a year later, here comes the judge. You know what I mean, divorce court."

"Well, Miss Meyer, since you are not here for divorce purposes, what can I do for you today?" Jacob asked.

"It's about Mr. Billings. I heard on the radio early this morning that he had been found dead, shot in the head, in your office. I got the telephone book, wrote down your address and here I am. You see, mister, can I call you Jacob?"

"You can call me Jacob, Miss Meyer, that's my name alright."

"Thank you, Jacob, you can call me Lucy. Well, my reason for being here is because I'm a neighbor of the late Mr. Billings. I live on

Coldwater Canyon, halfway up from the Hollywood side of the mountain. The last few days there has been a lot of going in and out at Mr. Billings' place. You see, the gate entrance to his house is like five feet away from my backyard patio. Every time someone opened and closed the gate, I could hear the metallic sound it made. I could also hear loud voices, men's voices, arguing about money. I don't know what Mr. Billings did for a living, but it must have paid him well, you know. Driving a new convertible Cadillac and having all these female visitors for swim parties in his pool. Sometimes it went on till all hours of the night."

"Did you see or hear anything unusual, Miss, excuse me, Lucy? You know, did someone threaten him with physical harm? Did you hear gun shots for instance?"

"I was coming to that, Jacob. I read several Raymond Chandler books, you know, where he has this Philip Marlowe as a detective. My intuition told me to keep an eye on things. I saw this car parked near the entrance for a few days. There was a rough looking man sitting behind the wheel, watching or waiting for somebody. I wrote down the license plate number just in case this individual did something wrong." Lucy handed a piece of paper to Jacob with scribbling on it.

"When did you last see the car with the man in it parked near the house?"

"It was just last night, Jacob. It was two in the morning and I was just about to go to sleep when I heard a noise that sounded like a firecracker. I got up and went to the side window without turning any lights on; that's when I saw two men, one on each side, carrying Mr. Billings to the car parked on the street. Poor Mr. Billings looked drunk, his head was down and he could not walk straight. The two men had to drag him."

"Did anyone see you looking at them, Lucy?"

"I don't think so, Jacob. They never looked in my direction and as I said, there were no lights on in my house. There is a street light right at the corner of my property and Mr. Billings.' I went back to bed not thinking anything of it, until this morning on the news where they announced that Louis Billings had been found dead on your office floor with a bullet hole in his head. I was going to call the police but then changed my mind."

"Why did you not call the police, Lucy, they need to know this information from you. When a person knows facts related to a crime, especially a murder, that person should inform the authorities. Why did you choose to tell me instead, Lucy?"

"I know about your reputation, Jacob. Two months ago, you did some investigation work for two friends of mine, the Campagnos who live in Studio City. They told me how good you are so I thought I could trust you better than the police," said a smiling Lucy Meyer.

"You flatter me, dear lady, so let's see where we are going with this." Jacob had to sort his thoughts for a moment, place them in an order that would make his questioning simple and to the point. "About these two men who were dragging Louis Billings from his backyard to the parked car, had you seen them on previous occasions, Lucy?"

"I don't think so, Jacob. I only saw a profile of two big men, you know six feet tall and muscular, didn't see their faces at all. I would have recognized them if they had been there before. You know, I'm very observant about what goes on in my neighborhood, Jacob."

Jacob thought for a moment how lucky Lucy Meyer had been for not turning the lights on. Her reading mystery novels probably saved her life. These characters don't like to leave witnesses behind, especially if a witness could identify them in some way. "Tell me, Lucy, was there anything else you observed either last night or before that could be important to this case? You know, I will have to inform Lieutenant Jones about the license plate, but don't worry, I'll keep your name out of it for now."

"Thank you, Jacob, I knew I could trust you. I won't mention our conversation to anyone else. No, I cannot think of anything further for the moment. If something comes up, may I call you?"

"You certainly may, Lucy, and here's my card with two telephone numbers. Thanks for coming to me, Lucy, I appreciate it."

Jacob got up and escorted Miss Meyer to the door. The building janitor had cleaned up his office floor and no trace of blood could be seen where slimy Louis' body had been dropped.

He picked up the telephone and dialed Lieutenant Jones' number. "Jacob Schreiber here, Lieutenant, do you think I could impose on you for a small favor? Normally I would use some other channel, but I need a real fast answer on this one. Could you find out who owns this plate number for me, Lieutenant? I'll owe you one if you do. It could be a stolen car too. One never knows."

"Not a problem, Jacob, let me have it," said a cheerful Bill Jones.

CHAPTER THREE...

Just as Jacob was placing the key to unlock his apartment door, he noticed an envelope sticking out from the bottom of the door. As he carefully opened the door, he bent down to pick up the envelope left there by someone. It had his name on the face of it, but he did not recognize the handwriting. The message inside was on a plain piece of paper and said for him to call Mark at the number written by 8:30 tonight. Jacob remembered Mark was a bartender in one of the bars on Sunset Boulevard near Doheny. It was a favorite hangout for bookies, pimps and two-bit actors. Before going to war, Jacob had saved Mark, whom he did not know at the time, from a severe beating at the hands of two thugs. Jacob's interference had chased the hoodlums away from Mark, who had suffered a broken nose and a black eye. He later found out Mark had been at the wrong place at the wrong time and was wearing the same type of clothing a certain bookie they had been looking for always wore. The hoods came back to the bar to apologize to Mark and gave him two C notes to replace his ruined clothing.

Jacob wondered about the message asking him to call. He checked his personal telephone book and saw it was the bar's number. Less than ten people knew where Jacob lived. Mark was one of them. It really did not matter in this modern era, one could easily find out someone's address if one had a mind to. Looking at his watch, he saw it was almost eight-thirty. Jacob went to the telephone and dialed the bartender's number. Soon he would know what this was all about.

The business must have been good because the telephone rang seven times before Mark answered. "This is Jacob Schreiber; you wanted me to call; what's up, Mark?"

"Hi, Jacob, I'm glad you called. Could you stop by tonight? I have some information about the guy who was found dead in your office.

Louis Billings I believe his name was. Interesting stuff I hear in this worldly place."

"I could be there in an hour, if it's convenient for you. Okay, see you then, Mark."

All of a sudden Jacob thought, *everybody has some news about the dead bookie that happened to be laid to rest in my working environment.* First there was Lucy Meyer, who confirmed in some way that Louis 'The Snake' had been murdered in his own house before being dumped in his office. There has to be some reason why Louis' body was taken to a private eye's office and not left where he had been killed.

With time on his hands, he picked up the telephone and called Helen Billings. Maybe he would get some answers from her and again, maybe not! This time after three rings Helen Billings answered.

"This is Jacob Schreiber, Mrs. Billings. Would you have a moment to talk with me?" the private investigator asked.

"Hi! Jacob, how in the world are you?" asked a tipsy sounding Helen. "I'm glad you called. Some police lieutenant was here earlier; his name was Smith, Brown or Jones; whatever, I can't recall. He wanted to know if I had killed old Louis. You know what, Jacob, I told him I wish I could have. Now I won't have to go to court. Isn't that wonderful, Jacob? Whatever the SOB did, he played with the wrong boys. When you're a bookie, there are some nasty, powerful and heartless people you have to answer to. I know all this because over the years Louis fed me his bullshit on a daily basis 'till I got rid of him. You know what I mean, threw him out of the house so to speak. I know I'm the one that left. It was not such a bad idea. I guess the house is mine now unless he changed his will and gave it to one of his bimbos. What's on your mind, Jacob?"

"Just thought I'd ask you if you have any idea who could have done away with your husband. Well, I guess Lieutenant Jones probably asked you that question already." Jacob realized by Helen Billings' voice she had been drinking more than usual. "Would you have any idea why his body was dumped in my office? He was not a client, but you were."

"Why don't you come by my place tomorrow, Jacob. I should feel better by then and we can talk about Louis' departure from the land of the living, face-to-face. Is 2 o'clock okay with you, Jacob?"

"I'll see you tomorrow at two, Helen." Jacob was confident that Helen, in her pretend naïveté, knew more than she let on. Now he could go to the bar on Sunset, have a talk with Mark and find out what he knows about the famous bookie's departure. All this was building up to something, but what? Jacob was not a gambler, therefore, no contacts with bookies. His only gambling was at the Hollywood Park racetrack once a month. He was not a drug user nor did he frequent prostitutes. Why would the body of a bookie, loan shark, pimp, and whatever else one does around the circles of the "high" rollers be dumped on his turf? What is the message here? Jacob was thinking. *Am I missing something, or was it done to confuse the police? You never know what to think when you have to deal with the underworld characters of today,* he thought. *Using a curve to hide the true reasons for a crime would be right up their alley. Try to make the cops think the gumshoe killed the guy and give themselves time to hide their tracks.* Jacob could not think of one reason why he was being used, aside from not being popular with mobsters.

As Jacob walked in the popular watering hole, he recognized a few shady characters he had previously seen at the local LAPD booking office. The cream of the sleaze, as he liked to call them, was sipping drinks, gossiping and making under-the-table deals. The atmosphere was dark and very smoky. He thought it smelled like the cigar store on Hollywood Boulevard where he regularly bought his morning paper. As he approached the bar, Mark greeted him with a nod of the head and motioned him to take the last barstool on the right.

"How is it going, Mark?" asked the anxious PI. "You look as if you have the right crowd tonight," Jacob said with tongue in cheek. "Are they all for real, or are some of these out of the Forest Lawn Mausoleum up the street?"

Mark answered with a smile as he knew what Jacob meant, and

slid a beer toward him on top of the shiny bar. "You won't believe what I heard about you a couple of nights ago. Louis Billings was here with two strangers. One looked like a has-been prizefighter and the other was an average height, well-dressed Mafia type with a New York accent. Louis was doing most of the talking at the time. He was complaining about his divorce coming up in court in a couple of weeks. He told these two thugs about you being hired by his ex to follow him all over the place. A real nuisance he called you. He even said you could be a fagot the way you walked. I had to laugh to myself. Jacob, if this idiot only knew about your abilities in martial arts, he wouldn't have said that. The well-dressed guy did all the asking. At one point, I heard him say, 'When will you have the ten grand, Louis?' 'Give me a week,' Louis answered. Then I heard the guy say that was not good enough. The boss and he referred to Black Jack Tony 'He wants his money now or you become fish bait, Louis.' That New Yorker had steel blue eyes that showed no emotions. He then told Louis he would give him two more days to get the cash. The two strangers got up and left without saying any more. Louis just sat there looking dejected. I had never seen him in this condition. He asked me if he could use the bar telephone and I told him it was okay. The guy really looked scared. I would have been too if I were in his shoes, Jacob," the barman concluded.

"It all sounds interesting, Mark, but without a name it would be too difficult for me to trace these guys. Black Jack Tony, on the other hand, is not the kind of person one betrays or crosses. I'll pass this information on to my friend Lieutenant Jones without your face on it," Jacob said.

Before Jacob could get up to leave the premises, Mark stopped him. "There's one more thing that happened the following night, Jacob. These two same characters came back to the bar with one other guy I have seen around here before. His name is Jack Paluka, a known enforcer for 'the family.' The three of them had a good time laughing aloud and mentioned Louis' name a few times. They even mentioned your name and thought it would be funny to see the expression on your face when you walked in your office in the morning. Paluka at one point said, 'Tony would be happy to see the snake gone. Nobody will know who did it. The gumshoe will have some explaining to do.' Then they all laughed again," concluded the bartender.

"You're sure, Mark, this was Jack Paluka, the owner of the pawnshop on Sunset and Western? If it is, I'm going to have some fun at his expense this time around. I know he's working for Black Jack Tony, otherwise he would never be able to operate his pawnshop. So, you think they're the ones who put Louis to sleep last night."

"Yes, Jacob, I am convinced these three guys, without a doubt, were the hit-party for one former bookie, pimp and sleaze ball. Furthermore, Jack made a call from the bar telephone and I heard him say, 'That's right, Tony, we'll dump him at the shamus' place.' Now if that's not convincing enough for you, I don't know what is, my friend!"

"Thanks for the information, Mark, and let's keep it between us." Jacob got up and left the smoky place. He was glad to walk outside to some kind of fresh air after spending the better part of an hour inside the bar. Tomorrow he would make a special visit to Jack Paluka's pawnshop.

The pawnshop on Sunset and Western was strictly a front for mob operations. Pimps and bookies came there to make drops of cash to Jack Paluka, who obviously was a 'banker' for Black Jack Tony. When Jacob walked inside the store, there were no customers. He could see behind the counter there was a door with a small sliding window in it. As he walked by that location, he heard a voice say, "What can I do for you today?"

Looking in the direction where the voice came from, Jacob did not bother to answer. This he knew would bring whoever was behind the voice out in the open.

"Hey, mister, I said what could I do for you; are you deaf or something?" asked a man who suddenly appeared behind the counter.

"I'm looking for an old guitar that was stolen from me one week ago. You wouldn't happen to have old guitars, would you?" Jacob asked in a nonchalant tone.

"I do have guitars," the man said. "How do I know it's yours? We don't carry stolen goods in our store, for your information."

"Cut out the crap and show me what you have. My name is embossed on it and I have ID's with me. Maybe I'll go back out and bring my brother in here. He's a lieutenant with the LAPD. I'm sure he'd love to look at your stolen merchandise."

"Now look here, buster," said the man, "the guitars are to your right, look all you want. I'll be right here watching you," the store owner said.

Jacob took his nonchalant walk and attitude in the direction the man had indicated. Turning around to face Paluka, Jacob said, "It doesn't look like you have my guitar anyway," turned around and walked right out the door. As he stepped on the sidewalk, he wondered who this sleaze ball would call to find out which LAPD lieutenant had a brother who played the guitar. He laughed all the way to his office.

CHAPTER FOUR...

Lieutenant Bill Jones was going over his notes on the Louis Billings case when his telephone rang. "Jones here," said a smiling voice. "Oh, it's you, Jacob. How is the private investigating business going? Any corpses to report?" said a cheerful detective. "What! You are inviting me for coffee and doughnuts? Are you sure you can afford this, shamus, or is it bribery you have in mind? I'll meet you on the pier in Santa Monica in an hour."

The lieutenant wondered what Schreiber had in mind. Did he find something relevant to the Billings murder case! He felt friendliness towards Jacob. What Jones liked about him was his discipline and honesty. He had never tried to hide facts from him on previous cases. For those reasons, the LAPD detective was ready to cooperate with this PI. The majority of private investigators he felt were scammers looking to make a fast buck the easy way. Not Jacob the straight shooter.

"I see you made it within the hour, with time to spare, Lieutenant," Jacob said. "Let's get a cup of coffee and a doughnut and take a walk down the end of the pier. I have some information you may want to look into about Louis 'The Snake,' the night before his disappearance. A friend, who shall remain nameless for now, called me last night with a story that could help you close this Billings case. The night before Louis was bumped off, he showed up at my friend's bar with two strangers. Most likely, import boys from New York or New Jersey to do the job. One looked like a beat-up ex boxer and the other was the suave Mafia type. The elegantly dressed guy did all the talking. The main subject of the conversation that my friend overheard was about ten grand Louis had to come up with, pronto! Louis wanted a week to come up with the cash, but the man gave him two days to get it or, according to Black Jack Tony, their boss, Louis would become fish bait! Interesting conversations these intellectuals always have, don't you think, Lieutenant?"

"I've heard better conversations at the morgue, Jacob. You said on the telephone someone had given you a license plate number. What is that all about? Would you mind filling me in?" asked the lieutenant.

"This woman, who happens to be a neighbor of our departed snake, was in my office late afternoon the same day you discovered the body. The night before Louis was found, she had heard some noises coming over the fence as she sat on her patio. Later that same night, after she had gone to bed, she heard sounds like firecrackers. She got up without turning the lights on, looked out the side window and saw two men holding Louis and dragging him towards a car parked near the curb under the light post. There was a third man in the car waiting for them. He got out and opened the back door so they could put Louis in. She thought that Billings was drunk or appeared to be drunk. I guess she didn't realize at the time Louis had been shot and was already dead. Because of where the car was standing, she was able to get the plate number, which she gave to me; this is the one I gave you over the telephone. From the description she gave me of the trio, I now know they were the two strangers from the bar on Sunset, and Jack Paluka, owner of a pawnshop on Sunset near Western. I assume he was the driver of the car. It could be his unless it was stolen for convenience."

"I'm afraid I'll owe you once again, Jacob. You seem to be making a habit of being one step ahead of me. I really don't mind because I trust your judgement. You and I understand each other, I wouldn't want it any other way. Anything else you could enlighten me with today? I wish you would join the force, you and I would make a great team. Not that we're not now, but working as two police officers would be great, don't you think so, Jacob?"

"Lieutenant, if the department could pay me what I make now, I would think about it. I enjoy the freedom of action I have you know. I am not ready to consider any offer at this time. You and I can keep on helping one another without too many choking rules to adhere to. Why don't you check out the plate number I gave you? I have the

THE BOOKIE

feeling it belongs to Jack Paluka. I was in his pawnshop late yesterday pretending to be looking for an old guitar. He's kind of a gruff guy. I told him if he didn't let me look for my guitar I would have my brother, a detective from the LAPD, pay him a visit. I don't think he appreciated that at all. He became very friendly all of a sudden. I'm sure he has a fear of the police. That's all I have for now, my friend; I hope it can help you in some way."

Jacob turned around to walk off the pier and get back to his car when he noticed a person he thought had a familiar look. As he got closer to the person leaning on the protective rail looking at the ocean, a picture came to his mind. Two years ago, in 1943, this familiar face had been with him in the South Pacific. Jacob searched his memory for a name. Then it hit him, Alexander Fitzsimmons was part of his platoon until he was wounded. Hit by a stray bullet in the leg, he remembered. Jacob approached the man and tapped him on the shoulder. "Alexander," he exclaimed, "good to see you. I didn't know you lived in southern California."

The man stared at Jacob for a moment, stunned as if he didn't recognize who was standing in front of him. "Jacob Schreiber," he said aloud. "My God, it's been some time since I last saw you. To answer your question first, yes, I have lived right here in Santa Monica for the past year. Did you ever fulfil your war dream of having your own investigating business, if I remember right?"

The two men hugged each other for a moment. Both stood back looking at the other as if it wasn't real. Two wartime friends who probably thought the other had died meet unexpectedly with great joy.

"Yes, Alex, I am living my dream. It's so rude of me; let me introduce you to Lieutenant Bill Jones of the LAPD. Lieutenant, this is Alexander Fitzsimmons. He and I served under the same commanding officer for a couple of years."

"Nice to meet you, Alexander. I'm sure your commanding officer had a hard time with both of you," said a smiling Lieutenant.

"Jones, Jones, our commanding officer was Colonel Jones, are you related to him?" asked Alexander.

"He was my brother. Octavio was killed in an automobile accident three months ago, when returning from San Francisco, I'm sorry to say."

The three men kept on walking towards the parking lot. The lieutenant waved to the two friends as he got in his car. Jacob was walking to his car, followed by Alexander, when he noticed one of the rear tires was flat. As he got closer, he saw it had been slashed. A note had been pinned to the rubber. 'Quit nosing around about Louis Billings' death, shamus. The next puncture could be you instead of a tire.'

"Can you believe that, Alex? Some punk slashed my tire. Now," Jacob said as he opened the trunk, "I'll have to get my hands dirty." He didn't tell his friend about the note.

Alex said, "There are always some beachbums around here who have nothing else to do but vandalize and damage other people's property. It can turn ugly if you catch them doing it, don't you think, Jacob?"

"I know what you mean, Alex. By the way, you didn't tell me what you have been up to since you left the Marines," Jacob asked.

"Three months after I was released I moved from San Diego to Santa Monica and opened an art shop. As you know, I had an art degree before the Marines came along. Aside from teaching a course on canvas, I also sell art paraphernalia and do custom framing. It was slow at first but once the people got to know me, I have been doing well. In fact, if you tell me where I can reach you, I'm going to send you an invitation to my wedding."

"Congratulations, Alex. Here's my business card with all you need on it. I'll be happy to come to your wedding. Who's the lucky girl?"

"Gabriella is her name. She's my highschool sweetheart. A very talented girl. She paints, designs, does pottery and is a great gardener. Not to mention her cooking abilities. Oh yeah, she's beautiful too."

After Jacob finished changing his tire, they parted company. The gumshoe headed for Studio City where he had promised a tipsy

THE BOOKIE

Helen Billings last night he would meet with her today. On his way up the Sepulveda pass, he switched to his thinking cap. Some people did not want him to find out something or other on sleazy Louis' activities. He knew the bookie was into several shady operations with underworld characters. What was it they did not want him to find out? His curiosity was aroused and besides, whoever it was had made it personal by dumping the body in his office, then slashing his tire and leaving a threatening note. That last part was all the motivation Jacob needed to pursue the matter. Maybe Helen Billings would bring some new light to an intriguing situation. One thing bothered him above all, the fact Black Jack Tony appeared to be involved in the demise of Louis 'The Snake.' Tony's reputation was well known amongst the criminal element of southern California. He was the ruthless big cheese. No one crosses Tony Padilla, cheats him and gets away with it. Some missing individuals never surfaced anywhere again. It was said his cement factory contained the solution to a few of those missing persons. Whatever Louis Billings did, it had to be big to cost him his life, ten thousand dollars was not enough. Unanswered was still the question of dumping his body at a PI's office who was not involved directly with Louis, indirectly if one considers the divorce procedures undertaken by Helen Billings. *This could be the key to the puzzle*, he thought as he pulled in front of Helen's house on Morella. As he approached the door, he could hear the bark of a large dog. So, she got herself a dog for protection. Not a bad idea when a woman lives alone.

CHAPTER FIVE...

It had been a long session with Helen Billings, three hours of mostly listening on Jacob's part. She had gone into ten years of Louis' activities as a bookie for the mob. Either she didn't know about his pimping or she just ignored it. His dealing in stocks was another aspect she only knew very little about. About five years ago Louis had a safe put in under the floor of the living room where the piano stood. A secured place he had told her. At the present time no one was living in the house, but Helen knew from the lawyer it would stay hers since the divorce proceedings had not started and Louis had no new will laying anywhere. Helen had gone to the house earlier in the day and took everything out of the hidden safe. She showed Jacob the contents. There were ten grand in cash, a paid life insurance policy for $100,000, with her as the beneficiary, and three other envelopes. She had given Jacob a large brown envelope containing papers that referred to the (upcoming) divorce proceedings.

When Jacob got back to his office, Anne had already left for the day but not without a few messages scribbled and placed in the middle of his desk for him not to forget. Two new possible clients, and Lieutenant Jones had called twice. He wondered what could be so urgent. He picked up the telephone and dialed the LAPD detective number.

"Lieutenant Jones, how can I help you?"

"I never thought you would still be at your desk at this time of the day, Lieutenant; this is Schreiber. You called earlier today."

"That I did, Jacob. I have some development that surfaced after I got back to my office from Santa Monica this morning. I would like to talk with you about them now, if you can. Could you meet me in an hour at the Cast Away Lounge on Wilshire near La Cienega?"

"It sounds real urgent, Lieutenant, and since I don't have a date tonight, I'll meet you there," Jacob said with a hint of humor.

THE BOOKIE

His private office door was wide open and as he lifted his sight, he saw the silhouette of what appeared to be a man behind the glass of the main office door leading to the hallway. Jacob touched his underarm to confirm his .45 was in place, just in case. Having a dead bookie dumped on your office floor gets your nerves a bit more sensitive than usual. He saw the silhouette lift an arm and then heard a loud knock on the door. "Come on in, it's unlocked," he said aloud.

A tall, about six foot two, man dressed in a well-made silk suit came walking in toward him. He appeared to be of Mediterranean decent.

He extended his arm and said, "I'm Leon Edwards, Mr. Schreiber. I did not know if you were going to be here given the time of day. I happened to be close by and decided to try my luck while my chauffeur waits for me downstairs."

"Well, Mr. Edwards, what can I do for you?" Jacob asked gently as he saw the man was using a cane for walking support. The gumshoe figured this man to be in his late sixties, early seventies. Aside from the slight limp, he appeared to be well preserved. Leon reached in his pocket and brought out a photograph he placed on the desk.

"This is my son Earl. He's thirty-four years old. Three months ago, he arrived in Los Angeles from Dallas. My family is in the oil business, Mr. Schreiber. Three weeks ago my son called to inform me he was going to San Francisco for a weekend visit. I have not heard from him since and I fear something bad has happened to Earl on his way to San Francisco. I would like to retain your services to help me find him." As he finished talking, Leon Edwards pulled an envelope out of his pocket and deposited it in front of Jacob on top of his desk. "There's five grand in there to begin your work. Should you need more, just call the number on this card and it will be delivered to you immediately. Are you able to help me, Mr. Schreiber?"

"It's not a question of am I able to help, Mr. Edwards. I will need more information from you about your son, his reason for being in Los Angeles and whom he associated with, if you know. Why did you not go to the police to file a missing person's report? Not that it matters, but was your son in some kind of illegal activity, Mr. Edwards?"

"Not what you may call illegal, Mr. Schreiber, but may I say socially unacceptable activities and relationships. My son is a homosexual and does not care who knows about it. I have learned to accept his illness, Mr. Schreiber; he is still my son and I cannot deny that. I have him on the board of directors of my company and because an annual meeting is coming up in less than a month, I need to contact him. My only concern is that he is alive and well, you know. Would you find Earl for me, Mr. Schreiber?"

"I'll do all I can, Mr. Edwards, beginning tonight. I have a meeting coming up shortly with a friend who happens to be a lieutenant in the LAPD. With the information you are leaving here, we might get lucky fast. Where can I call you in L.A. if I need to?"

"Take this card, Mr. Schreiber; it has the three telephone numbers where I can be reached. I look forward to hearing from you soon."

After the man left, Jacob had a quick look at the names and addresses his new client had left for him. He put the envelope containing the money in his pocket and left the office to meet with Lieutenant Jones. On his way, he kept trying to guess what Jones wanted to talk to him about that was so urgent. *Oh well*, he thought, *Bill Jones has a habit of being direct and to the point, so I'll soon find out.*

The Cast Away Lounge is your typical Hollywood neighborhood bar. Jacob walked into a dark smoky place with loud music and animated customers who had too much to drink or too many auditions at one of the casting studios. He spotted the lieutenant seated in a corner away from the noisy clientele. "Well, Lieutenant, fancy meeting you here," Jacob said. After getting himself a beer, he took a seat directly across from the detective. "So, you have some new development you wanted to share with me. I'm assuming it has to do with Louis Billings. Am I right, Lieutenant?"

"That you are, Jacob. Do you recall mentioning a lady living next door to Louis 'The Snake' who might have seen something going on?"

THE BOOKIE

"Yeah, I do, her name is Lucy Meyer. She's the one who gave me the information on the car and the license plate number."

The detective said, "That's the one. Nothing happened to her. The car she mentioned was found on Mullholland Drive with a body in the trunk. It had been stolen in Laguna Beach two weeks ago. The body is that of a bookie friend of Louis by the name of Jack Strings. From what we found on him and about him so far, he was to meet with Louis at his house the night Mrs. Meyer saw two guys carry what she thought was a drunk Billings to the stolen car. Now that throws out my theory about Louis being murdered in his own house, don't you think?"

"Not necessarily, Lieutenant. You see today I had a long interview with Helen Billings and let me tell you what she said. The night before Louis' body was found in my office, he had dinner with his wife at her house in Studio City. She said he was unusually friendly rather than being adversarial. They talked and drank two bottles of wine. He left somewhat tipsy shortly after 2 AM. We know his car was parked in his driveway. Lucy Meyer never mentioned she had heard Louis come home at that time. As a matter of fact, I recall her telling me she got up around one-thirty to check on the firecracker noise she had heard, thinking there was a party going on next door. She also said she went right back to bed. Therefore, it is plausible the person being dragged to the stolen car was this Strings character. The driver of the car, whoever he was, must have realized the person being brought to him was not Louis 'The Snake.' For that reason, Lieutenant, I assume they placed the body in the trunk and waited around for Louis to show up."

"What you're saying, Jacob, does make sense, but when did they snuff Louis out and why take his body all the way to your office? Unless they were looking for something there and took Louis to guide them. There was blood on the small carpet of your office and the lab says it was the bookie's blood. What's your theory on Louis being shot in your office?"

"I don't know, Lieutenant, it could have been that way. Only a few things were disturbed and no documents are missing. I still don't get the reason why my office was used. Louis was not a client, his wife was. Did you get to Jack Paluka, the owner of the pawnshop, yet?"

" I did, Jacob, and he has a good alibi for the night in question. Paluka is a shrewd one. We know he's a front for Tony Padilla. Someday he'll slip and we'll be all over him. I have assigned one of my plainclothes officers to keep an eye on who goes in and out of his store. I'll keep a vigil going for a few weeks. It may turn out something! This Jack Strings, do you know anything about him, Jacob? I cannot figure out why he would have your business card in his pocket. Did he have an appointment coming soon?"

"Never heard of him before, Lieutenant. Are you sure this is his legal name? You know these bookies use pseudonyms to protect their families and themselves for that matter. People making bets with Billings only knew him as Louis 'The Snake.' I would not be surprised if this Jack Strings has a different name on his driver's license. Did you not find a wallet on him when he was taken out of the trunk of the stolen car?"

"For whatever reason, Jacob, dead bodies keep showing up telling us they have some connection to you. My brother Octavio, bless his soul, vouched for your honesty when I first told him about a new gumshoe on the block. You and I understand each other well, and that is why I cooperate with you and you with me. This Jack Strings' real name was David Ross, a small time, all-around crook who operated a newsstand in Santa Monica. I see your eyebrows lifting, does the name David Ross ring a bell?"

"It does, Lieutenant. If I recall, I have an appointment with a person by that name tomorrow before noon. Now if that turns out to be this David Ross, I don't know what to say at this time, Lieutenant. A dead bookie, who is not my client, turns up dead in my office. Then, another dead bookie is found in the trunk of a car with my card in his pocket and he happens to be, I assume, a prospective client. If the trend keeps up, I won't be in business long! Prospects are supposed to stay alive until they become clients and leave a retainer with me. There has to be a connection between these two dead

THE BOOKIE

bookies and me. I don't know what it is yet, but the moment I find out, Lieutenant, you'll be the first to know." Jacob was a bit perplexed. He wasn't sure what the lieutenant wanted or where he was going with the conversation. "Since we are on the subject of names, does the name Earl Edwards bring anything to mind, Lieutenant?"

"Earl Edwards, no matter how I turn it in my head, Jacob, no red flags anywhere. Is it supposed to remind me of someone?"

"I hope not, but I'll let you know when I find out where he is and if he's still alive. Is it possible for you to check the missing persons and let me know? Can I buy you one more before I go, Lieutenant?"

"I'll take a rain check, Jacob. I have a busy day tomorrow trying to sort out these bodies that drop all over the place."

CHAPTER SIX...

As he left the bar, Jacob noticed someone trying very hard not to be seen following him. He turned and went back to the bar. The lieutenant was just on his way out. When he saw Jacob, he had an inquisitive look on his face.

"Lieutenant, I need you to do me a favor, if you don't mind! There's a guy outside who was trying his best to follow me. When I first noticed him, he was leaning on an old black four door Dodge. He's about my size and wears a beige jacket, no tie and dark trousers. Why don't you check him out and I'll just keep on walking by."

"Happy to do so, Jacob," said the detective. "Call me later, I'll let you know who it was," he said as he left through the front door.

Jacob waited a couple of minutes and proceeded on his way. As he passed by the lieutenant, he had the man spread eagle and was frisking him. He smiled, but kept on walking to the next street where his car was parked. The night was still young, but he had some reading to do, so he headed for his office. He sat at his desk thinking about the events of the last days. The envelope Helen Billings had given him was there in the In basket. He grabbed it and dumped the contents on the desk. Mostly papers related to the divorce investigation Jacob had done some months earlier. Amongst the papers was a small envelope that caught his attention, it was sealed with nothing written on the outside. He decided to open it to find out what was in there. After reading the contents, he let out a long whistle. *Wow,* he thought, *no wonder this guy was eliminated. With what he knew, he was a danger to the mob's plan.* Still, Jacob had a feeling there was more to what he had just read. He would have to contact Helen Billings to see if she would cooperate and let him go through all of Louis' personal files. The ring of the telephone startled him. It was almost 10 PM. "Schreiber here," Jacob answered.

"It's Jones, Jacob, wanted you to know your potential tail is one

THE BOOKIE

of Black Jack Tony's stable boys. I confiscated his piece, a cheap 9mm he must have picked up from a war surplus store downtown. I also had a patrol officer give him a ticket for illegal parking, which won't help him cool his hot head. You see, he was not illegally parked; either he pays the fine or he will have to go to traffic court, which I doubt he will do. He was in a hurry. The man kept telling me I was holding him back from a very urgent appointment. To make it short, I delayed him long enough for you to get away. Now we're even again as favors go. What are you doing so late in your office, Jacob?"

"Had nothing better to do, I guess, Lieutenant. I have something here I would like to share with you, but don't rush; it can wait until tomorrow."

Jacob went to his safe and placed the five grand he had received from Leon Edwards earlier and Louis Billings' little white envelope in there. Now, Jacob was beginning to see the larger picture. Prominent people such as the mayor were somehow connected to Black Jack Tony's illegal prostitution and drug operations. He turned the lights out, locked the door and left the building.

When Jacob entered his office the following morning, a constant ring of the telephone greeted him. He wished Anne would come in earlier than 10 AM, but this was his arrangement and he had to live with it. He picked up the telephone and with a tone of sarcasm answered, "Jacob Schreiber here, at your service, you name it, I do it, investigation that is."

"We are in a joyful mood this morning, are we not, Jacob? After you hear what I have to say, you may change your tune. This is Bill Jones. I don't know what kind of a magnet you carry Jacob, but you seem to be attracting a lot of attention lately. Unfortunately, the 'attractees' are from the other side of the track so to speak. If I didn't know better I would have you arrested and place in protective custody. You see, my friend, your name keeps popping up in the wrong places. Shortly after we left the Cast Away last night, an associate of Jack Paluka was found dead in Westwood near the

UCLA campus. He had been shot in the head by what appears to be a small caliber revolver. He was one of the loan sharks who dealt with Padilla's gang through Paluka. He had a paper in his pocket with your name badly scribbled on it. Did you know Terry Downs as a client, or was he someone who had something to do with one of your clients?"

"Well, Lieutenant, you sure know how to make a person's day. The only Terry Downs I know of, if this is the one, was a guy I met briefly when I was being released from the Marines. He approached me for conversation while we were waiting for hours just to sign a piece of paper. The only reason I remember him is that his left arm was cut off at the elbow. He told me he was defusing a booby-trap when it blew up on him and tore his arm away. I do remember telling him I was going to fulfill my dream and open my own business. I must have told him what kind of business I was planning to go into. Is he the same dead guy you are talking about, Lieutenant?"

"From the description you just gave me, Jacob, he's the guy alright. Did you ever see him again after your release?"

"Not a chance, Lieutenant. I was only being polite to a wounded war veteran at the time. I didn't like his approach or his style of conversation. Always mentioning how easy it is to make a fast buck in L.A. I wonder why he had my name written on paper? The type of people he hung around with would not have been too pleased to find out he knew me. Again, he may have wanted to reach me for a reason unknown to anyone. You know, Lieutenant, sometimes criminals have a period of remorse and want to confide in someone they can trust." Jacob held his thoughts for a moment, hoping his detective friend would say something. At this point, he could not think of any reasons why this Terry Downs would want to consult with him. "Did you find out anything else on Downs before you called me? I really can't remember anything else, Lieutenant. By the way, when you have time, come by my office and I'll show you what I mentioned I found last night."

"Thanks for the conversation, Jacob. I'll touch base with you later today if I can."

THE BOOKIE

Jacob sat behind his desk and began again to think about the events of the last few days. How fast things had happened. Three dead bodies in some way connected to a common work environment and criminal activities, and dangerous ones at that! He picked his unopened mail from the In basket. He tossed them back one by one until a plain white envelope with his name written by hand and misspelled caught his attention. As he reached for his metal letter opener, he wondered who could this be from. There were three small snap shots of three different people, the kind one takes at an amusement park. Not the best of quality but good enough to identify someone. On the back of each one was a name printed in black ink. Then a note which said, 'Call me if you want to know more. There's money in here for you,' followed with a Hollywood telephone number. The signature at the bottom is what made him speak aloud. "What the hell is going on here?" At the same time, Lieutenant Jones walked in the open door.

"Are you talking to yourself now, Jacob?" asked a startled detective.

"Wow, how did you get here so fast, Lieutenant? I just talked to you minutes ago, or was it longer? These dead bodies showing up in my office or with my name written on a paper carried by them has me intrigued. Take a seat, Bill. Let me show you what made me speak loudly as you were walking in." He handed the note with the pictures to the lieutenant.

"Terry Downs sent this to you before he was snuffed out. Someone must have known he was trying to reach you with damaging information. I recognize two of the photos here, but don't know who the third one is."

"The puzzle is getting bigger day by day, Lieutenant. I don't think I want to touch this any further, so I'll leave it in your capable hands. If it were a client, there is no way I would share all this information with you until I could come to a satisfactory conclusion as to who is behind these murders. I am being used and I don't know why. That bothers me more than being threatened."

"Have a cup of coffee, Jacob. I bought two next door with a

couple of doughnuts, take your pick. By the way, you told me last night you had found something I should have a look at, is this it?"

"No, Lieutenant, that was not it." Jacob got up and walked to his wall safe, turned the combination, retrieved a white envelope with no writing on it and handed it to the detective. "What's in that envelope is what I found last night as I was going through a larger envelope filled with my investigation reports on Louis 'The Snake' for Helen Billings. She gave me the envelope yesterday, said she had no need for it now. She said she had gotten it from Louis' safe in his house. Since he's dead, and did not change his will, her lawyer told her the house and contents were hers because the divorce did not happen. This envelope was sealed so Helen Billings would not know its content. What do you think, Bill; will this help you in any way to solve these murders?" asked an anxious gumshoe. Jacob then reached for the doughnut and coffee.

Lieutenant Jones said, "You sure came up with some unusual events, or is it the other way around this time? I still don't have a motive for the three musketeers at the morgue, Jacob. There is no quick fix to this triple murder. Three bookies all involved in other illegal activities aside from book making. There has to be a common denominator somewhere. It must be within those photographs and papers you just handed me."

"Well, Lieutenant, if I find more hidden treasures, I'll turn them over to you. In fact, I may be able to get to Louis' personal files. If I do, there may be some material of interest for you. It's beginning to look larger than just a bookie being bumped off because he didn't pay his dues. When you have photos of the mayor of Los Angeles and the local congressional representative showing up in a hidden file, it smells of extortion. Would you not agree?"

"Yes I do, or a ring of high stakes betting along with well paid prostitutes who cater only to high profile men. I cannot disagree with you. Someone amongst the group of 'suppliers of sin' got greedy and wanted more than was offered. If there are no more corpses in the next few days, we will know the greed problem has been stopped. Hot times ahead, my friend!"

THE BOOKIE

"Well, Lieutenant, I have some other avenues to pursue. Did you find anything on Earl Edwards as I asked you yesterday?"

"Shucks, Jacob, I'm sorry, I almost forgot, here's where and with whom this young man associates. I understand his father is a rich oilman. He hangs around a group of actors that we are keeping an eye on. There have been some rumors of pornography involving children. From what I hear, this Edwards boy is as queer as a three-dollar bill. One of the detectives on the morality squad gave me the information when he heard me mention Earl Edwards. Just be careful when you make contact with the group. They have some tough muscle boys as bodyguards. Just a friendly warning, Jacob."

"Thanks again, my friend, let's keep in touch," Jacob concluded as he took the information sheet from the lieutenant.

CHAPTER SEVEN...

Anne Dombrowski had decided to come to the office early on this day. She was expecting some relatives to arrive from Germany in late afternoon. Eight AM was an unusual time for her to be there. She was just looking over the morning paper when the telephone rang. "Jacob Schreiber Investigation services, this is Anne, how can I help you?" she said. A distressed voice was mumbling at a speed Anne could not follow. "Slow down, lady, I cannot understand what you are trying to tell me. I can't help you if I don't know what you want," said a calm secretary.

"I'm scared, my husband... I mean my ex-boyfriend has threatened to kill both my son and me. I'm telling you he's crazy. I don't know what to do," a trembling voice said.

"The first thing you could do is give me your name and address and telephone number," Anne asked. "You could also call the police and make it an emergency."

"I've call the police before, but they show up after he's gone. I don't know where he lives so I can't tell them. A friend told me about Mr. Schreiber and how good he is at finding people and making things right. Could I come and see him now? Oh yeah! My name is Lorraine Buford and I live at 1800 North Kingsley Drive, apartment seven." She then gave Anne her telephone number and said she would be in the office in a half-hour.

Anne did not have time to tell Lorraine Buford that Jacob had not arrived at the office yet. Something must have held him up. Jacob was known to be in his office before eight in the morning, and sometimes he stayed very late at night. The life of a private eye was not always as glamorous as depicted in popular detective novels. She was just finishing reading the newspaper headlines when the famous gumshoe walked in, coffee in hand. He had a surprised look on his face when he realized Anne was in.

"Good morning, mister detective," said a cheerful sounding secretary. "Your telephone sure rings a lot this early in the morning, did you know that?"

"Well, what have I done to have the pleasure of your presence at such an ungodly hour of the day? And good morning to you, Miss Dombrowski," said a jestering Jacob. "Any interesting phone calls I should know about?"

"Yes there is," Anne replied. "A Lorraine Buford is going to be here shortly. She has a serious problem with an ex-boy friend. My feeling is that she should go to the police, but she said she has done that route with no results. She mentioned a friend you did some work for recommended she get in touch with you to help her solve her problem."

Jacob went to his desk, placed his coffee on top of the blotter, his morning paper on the corner and walked back to the office safe. He took out the envelope containing the five thousand dollars Leon Edwards had left with him. He walked to Anne's desk, handed her the envelope and said, "Would you mind making a bank deposit for us this morning? We have a new client by the name of Leon Edwards from Dallas, Texas. His address and telephone numbers are on top of the envelope. He wants me to look into the whereabouts of his thirty-four-year-old son Earl Edwards, who he has not heard from in several weeks. According to Edwards senior, the son came to Los Angeles a little over three months ago to visit some friends. He usually called every week to let his father know where he was and what he was doing. Leon has not heard from Earl recently and is worried because the annual meeting of the board of directors of his oil company is coming up soon and he needs to have his son there. That should give you enough information to begin your file." As he walked back to his private office, he heard someone come in the front door.

Anne got up and greeted the woman. "You must be Lorraine, am I right?" said the secretary.

"Yes you are, is Mr. Schreiber in yet, and could I see him?"

"Let me inform him that you're here, Miss Buford; just take a seat for a moment, I'll be right back," Anne said. She walked into Jacob's office and told him Lorraine Buford was here to see him. "She appears a little distressed, so go easy with her, Jacob." Anne, being some three years older than Jacob, now and then liked to give him motherly advice, especially when it came to female clients who either appeared or sounded distressed.

"Bring her in, it doesn't look as if she brought her son with her. I'll see if I can do anything for her. Could you call Lieutenant Jones and ask him where I could meet with him in about an hour from now?"

"You can come in now, Miss Buford," Anne said as she walked out of her boss's office. "Mr. Schreiber is ready to see you," she said with a smile.

"Good morning, Miss Buford it is, I'm Jacob Schreiber. Tell me the problem you have and I'll see what I can do for you," said a relaxed gumshoe.

"My problem started about two months ago when I told my boyfriend Ron he had to get out of my apartment. He wasn't working, didn't look for work and hung around with some bums he called his friends. I told him he could go live with his friends. I made enough money to care for my son and myself but did not want to support him. Besides, he drank too much. When he drank, he became violent towards both Gerald and me. I had enough of his antics and kicked him out. Had my door lock and telephone number changed. He had made some long distance calls to the Midwest, which I had to pay for. The guy is a lost cause. I'm sorry it took me so long to see it. Now that he's left, he's been threatening me and my son almost on a daily basis. I'm scared, Mr. Schreiber"

"Did you not report this to the police, Miss Buford?"

"I did, twice. And twice they showed up after he had left. I showed the police officer the bruises I had on my face, arms and legs, but he didn't seem to care one way or the other. It has gotten to a point where I am thinking of getting a gun for my own protection. My son Gerald is nine and does not need to see his mother being hit by a no good.... You see, my husband was in the Marines. He was killed when the Japanese attacked Pearl Harbor. He was a gentle man. At six foot four, 235 pounds, he was a giant of a man. Our relationship was one of love and respect from both sides. I need your help, Mr. Schreiber, but I don't know how I am going to pay you for your services. I really don't have much to spare money wise with a growing boy."

"I'll tell you what I can do, Miss Buford. You see, I was in the Marines too and went to the South Pacific, but contrary to your husband, I was lucky and came back. In respect for your husband's courage and bravery, I'm going to charge you one dollar. Yes, to make it legal, just one dollar."

Lorraine Buford started to cry and thanked him at the same time. Jacob was a bit embarrassed and didn't know what to do or say. There was a knock at his door that saved the day. "Please come in," Jacob said.

"Lieutenant Jones is on the telephone and would like to speak with you, Jacob." Seeing Lorraine Buford crying, Anne said, "Is there anything I can do to help?"

"Would you be kind enough to get Miss Buford a coffee, and bring one for you and me at the same time." Jacob picked up the telephone and greeted the lieutenant. "What's up? So you can't meet me this morning. Are you able to get away for lunch? Good, meet me at the Wilshire Country Club at 1 o'clock," Jacob concluded. "Sorry about the telephone, Miss Buford. Here's my secretary back with the coffee. Now, I will need from you the full name of your ex-boyfriend. And you said he drives a car, do you know the make and license number by chance? Good. When he showed up at your place the last couple of times, was it always at a specific given time? Therefore, early evening seems to be his pattern when it comes to harassing you. Did he ever disturb you late at night or even in the middle of the night? I need your full address, also where you work, where your boy goes to school and how he gets there. Oh yes, the telephone numbers where I can reach you. Let me assure you before you go that once I find this individual he will never bother you again, or my name is not Jacob Schreiber."

"Thank you, Mr. Schreiber, I don't know what else to say. I don't mean to be a burden or sound like a beggar, but I had no other place to turn to and no one else I could trust. Now I have to leave and go to work. You have my number at work if you need to talk to me. Thanks again."

After Lorraine Buford had left, Jacob opened the bottom right hand drawer on his desk and pulled out a book that looked like a year-end school book. It was a roster of the Marine Corps members who had died in action during the war. As he turned the pages looking for the name Buford, he found it on page forty-two; Buford, Charles Henry, killed during the Japanese attack on Pearl Harbor. He was only thirty-one years old. In finding that Miss Buford had spoken the truth, Jacob had just convinced himself that he was going to find that creep, that coward who found his strength in beating up a defenseless woman. Let's see how he reacts to a man giving him the same treatment he gave to Lorraine Buford. Jacob couldn't wait to find the guy. He hated the slime balls that picked on women, especially when they had been drinking. He thought for a moment he might use the help of the lieutenant for this one. He certainly did not want to jeopardize his license privileges. This type of individual was on the same level as a pimp as far as he was concerned. He called Anne in and gave her the information he had obtained from Lorraine Buford. When he told her about his one dollar fee, Anne looked at him straight in the eye and smiled. No words needed to be spoken.

"While you were talking with Miss Buford, Leon Edwards called to ask if you would check a residence in Beverly Hills, here's the name and address. Edwards said he had heard from a friend that his son Earl might be spending some time at this person's estate. He wanted you to check it out today if you could and call him back once you did."

"Thanks, Anne, I don't know what I would do without you. I'll be at the Wilshire Country Club having lunch with Lieutenant Jones today. Since I have some time ahead of me, I'm going to take a tour of Beverly Hills. I may get lucky and find Earl Edwards. That would be the fastest and easiest money I have ever earned."

Surprises were in the air. Jacob Schreiber had a few coming his way.

CHAPTER EIGHT...

Jacob was driving south on Doheny towards Beverly Hills, where he hoped to find Earl Edwards. He was not expecting a rough environment, but one never knows. His Marine training and wartime action had prepared him well for this kind of work. Being alert is important in the private investigation business. In divorce cases he sometimes had to get physical with a guy who didn't like being caught cheating on his wife. Getting your picture taken in any kind of compromising situation was the right ingredient to lose your temper. Jacob found that out the fast way. His first case was one of those. As a rookie, he paid the price with a bloodied nose and a sore jaw for a few days. Now he was more alert and twice as careful. As he was driving, he kept his eyes on the street signs. When he got to Gregory, he made a right turn and went to the street number Anne had written down for him. He parked a couple of houses before the one he was looking for, turned the engine off and thought for a moment about what he would say. He got out of the car and walked towards 988. When he got there, the gate was locked, but there was an intercom on the pillar to the right. He rang and waited for an answer. He had to ring twice before someone's voice came on and said, "Who is there, please?"

"My name is Jacob Schreiber. I understand Earl Edwards is here."

The voice came back, "He was until a week ago; Earl and Mr. Bill went on a trip to San Francisco. They should be back tomorrow. Would you like to leave a number where they can call you?"

"No thanks, I have the number, I'll call Earl tomorrow." Jacob walked away and stepped along the bushes, waiting to see if someone would come to the gate and investigate the caller. After five minutes, no one showed up and he went back to his car. He drove north on Doheny, made a right on Wilshire and proceeded towards the country club. When he arrived he found his usual parking space and went inside. As a member of the club, he had reserved a table in the dining room and informed the headwaiter he was expecting a guest, Lieutenant Bill Jones of the LAPD, homicide division. Giving a name with a title always made an impression on the staff and Jacob knew it. The waiter gave him a corner table far enough away from the earshot of listeners. This way, he and his guest could have a private conversation without being afraid of being overheard by anyone. Within a few minutes, the detective arrived. "Glad to see you could make it, Lieutenant," said a smiling Jacob.

"I just wanted to see how the upper side of society lives on a daily basis," Jones answered, tongue in cheek. "You sure know how to pick your spots, Jacob. Don't you have to be a member to come here?"

"You do, Lieutenant. When I came back from the South Pacific, my mother and brothers wanted to give me a special gift, the life membership. Besides, Lieutenant, I'm not such a bad golfer when I put my mind to it. It is a nice place to have a quiet lunch. I have used it sparingly and only with special people."

After they had ordered, Jacob brought up the problem of Ron Bastion (Lorraine Buford's former boyfriend) and his threats on this war widow. After he told Jones the story, he gave him the license plate number and make of the car. "I need to know where this guy lives, fast. This low life individual has to be made aware that we have laws in our society that protect people from having their lives threatened. If my explanations don't work, I'll arrange to bring him to you for a refresher. Is that agreeable with you, my friend?"

"Maybe you can find something that he has done wrong or even looks close to being wrong. A few days in police custody may show him the light! By the way, about your other client Earl, what was his last name? Oh yeah, Edwards. I found out he was staying in Beverly Hills with an actor and a garment designer. Here's the address." The lieutenant handed Jacob a piece of paper. "My reason for wanting to see you is that one of my investigators heard from one of his stoolies that Paluka, you know, the pawnshop owner, is about to place a bounty on your head. Why he wants to do that, we don't know. Just wanted you to be informed so you could keep an eye on who is coming behind you. I have a feeling it's because of your snooping into Louis The Snake's affairs. There must be something they are trying very hard not to bring in the open. Drugs, guns or the movement of prostitutes, you name it, it could be one of the three or all for that matter. I personally lean towards the illegal sale of guns. Recently there has been a number of break-ins at different military depots across the country. Machine guns, small arms and ammunition were stolen from these premises. It has not been publicized yet, but as I said, I lean towards that because the underground market is rapidly growing for this kind of merchandise now that the war is over. What do you think, Jacob?"

"I don't know, Lieutenant, but thanks for the tip. I'll try to keep my back covered." Jacob was in deep concentration for a moment and did not hear the waiter address him until the lieutenant clicked the water glass with his spoon. The gumshoe looked up and realized the waiter was telling him he had a telephone call at the service desk. He excused himself and went to the telephone. "Jacob Schreiber," he answered.

"This is Anne, Miss Buford called and said that when she went home for lunch she noticed her ex-boyfriend's car parked in front of her apartment house. He was sitting in it with some other man she could not see. Jacob, she was terrified."

"Thanks, Anne, I'll look after it right now." The private eye went back to the table and explained to the lieutenant what was going on. He mentioned he would have to cut his lunch short and investigate the situation.

"Don't have to do that, Jacob. Let me call the office and have a patrol car show these guys what law enforcement is all about." Jones got up and went to the parking lot where his car was. On the police band radio, he gave the address where the car was parked along with the make and license number. He informed the patrol officers to be careful, as these individuals were dangerous and could be armed. He instructed to have them arrested, the car towed away and he would deal with it later today. The lieutenant returned to the table with a grin on his face. "Well, Jacob, these two characters won't disturb anyone for the next 24 hours or more," and he proceeded to tell his friend what he had done. They both had a good laugh and continued their more important conversation about gun trafficking.

It was almost 3 o'clock by the time they left the country club, each in his own direction. Jacob was smiling to himself as he drove back to his office. Sometimes lunches accomplished better results than official meetings in a Spartan environment. He ran up the two flights of stairs to his office. As he opened the door, Anne was just finishing a note to inform him she had to leave early to meet her incoming relatives from Germany at LAX.

"I got a second call from Miss Buford. She was laughing so hard it took her a couple of minutes to regain her composure to tell me what happened. She said that after she had called me, she stayed out of the way near the entrance to a drug store, keeping an eye on Ron and whoever was with him. All of a sudden, she said, three police cars arrived with sirens blasting. The officers all had their guns out and ordered the two guys out of the car with their hands up in the air. They made them go to the pavement face first, their legs spread apart. One officer searched them and appeared to have found something illegal in Ron's pockets. To make a long story short, they were both handcuffed, arrested and the car towed away. She was elated and figured you had something to do with it. Did you, Jacob?"

"No," Jacob said with a grin, "I wouldn't do that, but the lieutenant did." And he burst out in a loud laugh. "Now Jones and I are going to pay them a visit in their new quarters. They will both find out you do not mess with a war hero's widow. Exactly what will happen, I don't know yet, but you can be reassured these two low life people will not ever harass Miss Buford and her son again. Go get your relatives and take the day off tomorrow, Anne. If I get in trouble, I'll call you."

Jacob sat at his desk and pondered what the lieutenant had told him about Paluka. He picked the telephone and dialed Helen Billings' number. She answered after three rings. "This is Jacob

Schreiber again. I was wondering if I could come have a talk with you. What I would like if you agree is to look around Louis' former residence. I have a hunch I may find something that will tell me why he was murdered," Jacob concluded.

"Come on up anytime, Mr. Schreiber," Helen said. "I'll have the keys to the house ready for you. I do have a briefcase that he forgot the night he got himself sent to the Promised Land. You can have that too. I trust that if you find something of value, you will let me know."

"Thanks, Mrs. Billings, I'll come up in about an hour if it's okay with you."

When Jacob arrived at Helen Billings' place, she handed him the briefcase, which was locked, and the keys to Louis' former residence. She told him she had to have a cleaning crew, as the place was a terrible mess when she went to look at it.

"You know, Mr. Schreiber, I placed the house on the market. I don't want to live where he had his floozies and God knows who else around the damn place. Besides, he probably was murdered in the house and too many people from his old bookie crowd knew where he lived. I don't want to have surprises at all hours of the day or night for that matter."

Jacob thanked Helen Billings and left with the keys and the locked briefcase. His first inclination was to proceed to Louis' house. Without hesitation, he went directly there. Hopefully Lucy Meyer, the neighbor, would not see him arrive. He didn't feel like explaining his being there. When he arrived on Louis' street, he parked two houses down so as not to excite Miss Meyer's curiosity. Except for children playing on the sidewalk, no one else was around. He got out of the car and walked towards Louis' place. As he approached, he noticed the curtains were drawn closed. The lawn and front garden had been cared for. A real estate sign was on the lawn with a note "By appointment only." *So,* Jacob thought as he walked up to the front door, *Helen Billings wanted to bring a quick close to this part of her life.* He placed the key in the lock, turned and opened the door. Now if he could only find something of interest the lieutenant could use. He walked in and locked the door behind him.

Helen had told him there were three or four boxes stacked in what was supposed to be a linen closet. She saw they were full of papers and did not bother searching further. Jacob looked everywhere else in the house but could not find any other item of interest except for the boxes, which he decided to take with him. They were small enough for him to carry in one arm. As he left the front door walking towards the sidewalk, he noticed a car parked across the street with a guy in it who was trying his best not to be seen. He obviously did not succeed. Jacob made a mental note of the license plate and kept going to his car as if nothing had disturbed him. He drove towards the parked car, his window open. As he got to it, he slowed right down, pulled out his .45, pointed it directly at the man's head, and yelled "bang!" The thug got scared and pulled away from the curb as fast as he could in the opposite direction. *Now*, Jacob thought, *if they want to play hardball, I'll show them what it's all about.*

CHAPTER NINE...

Lorraine Buford showed up at Jacob's office unannounced with her son Gerald. "Good morning, Miss Anne," she said. "Gerald and I want to thank you for helping us with the problem we had. Do you think we could see Mr. Schreiber too?"

"Give me a moment to talk with him, I'll be right back." Anne walked in Jacob's office and told him that Lorraine Buford and her son Gerald were here to see him if he had a moment.

"I do, Anne, bring them right in," said a smiling gumshoe.

"Well, what have we got here?" Jacob said as he got up and shook young Gerald's hand. "I bet you would be a good baseball player. I'm Jacob Schreiber. You must be Gerald," said the private eye.

"Nice to see you again, Miss Buford. Now that this certain individual was caught with illegal drugs on him, you can rest for the next ten years, if not more. Judges are very strict when it comes to drug dealings. They'll throw the book at someone caught doing it."

"I came here to thank you, Mr. Schreiber, and pay you the fee I owe you," said a happy faced Lorraine.

"As I said before, one dollar will do it. You see, my friend the lieutenant did it all and since the city pays his wages, it works well all around, don't you think?"

"Here's your dollar and I want you to know I feel bad about not paying any more." She handed Jacob a dollar bill.

"Don't even think about it. An agreement is an agreement. Here, young man, you can have this dollar if you promise me you will take care of your mother."

"Are you a real gumshoe?" Gerald asked as he pocketed the money. His eyes were all over the place, looking at pictures of Marines Jacob had hung on the walls. "Do you carry a gun?"

"Now, Gerald, Mr. Schreiber is a busy man and does not need to answer all your silly questions," said an embarrassed mother.

"Not silly at all, Miss Buford. Yes I carry a gun, Gerald, to protect people like you and myself against criminals. The police department has given me a license to do so. See that frame on the wall, that's my authorization. Would you like to see my gun?" Jacob knew the young man would not refuse this kind of offer. He emptied the chamber and took the magazine out.

"Oh! Yeah, I sure would. I know my dad carried a gun too during the war." Gerald's eyes were as big as could be. His mother just sat there with a smile on her face. She was happy to see her son interact with a man approximately his father's age.

"Here, Gerald," Jacob said as he handed the empty gun to the young man. "One thing you must know about guns, they can be dangerous if in the hands of someone with bad intentions. Never point a gun at someone unless you intend to shoot that person. When I did my basic training with the Marines, that's what they taught us. Always point a gun in the direction you intend to shoot. It's a bit heavy to hold, but since I carry it in my shoulder holster all the time, I don't feel the weight." Young Gerald handed the gun back to Jacob, who automatically reloaded it and placed it in its holster. "Do you play baseball, young man?"

"He doesn't really," said the mother. "You see, he hasn't made too many friends since we moved to Hollywood. I'm sure he would like to if there was some team he could be on."

"Well, if you really want to play, I may have a spot on my team for you. How old did you say you were?"

"I was nine years old two weeks ago, sir. You really have a baseball team with kids on it?" asked an excited boy.

"You see, Gerald, in my spare time I manage a Little League team in Griffith Park. We start training next week; would you like to come over and meet the other kids?"

"Now, Mr. Schreiber, you really don't have to do that."

"I know I don't have to, but I want to. Does Gerald have a glove?"

"I have a glove, sir. My dad bought it for me when I was little. I have a baseball too and a bat," said a sparkling faced Gerald. "Yeah, Mom, I could go play if you drive me there, would you?"

THE BOOKIE

"It's not a problem for me to take you to the park as long as you listen well to Mr. Schreiber's instructions. When exactly is your team meeting?" asked an elated mother. She could not believe what this man was offering to her son. The last few months had been difficult on Lorraine and then because she decided to do something about an existing problem, everything changed for the better.

"Let me give you this application. Its very simple, just fill out what they ask and bring it with you next Tuesday at 5 o'clock. You know where the baseball diamond is. I'll make sure he stays on my team."

After Lorraine and Gerald left the office, Anne walked in. "What did you do to these folks? They walked out of here as if they were floating on a cloud."

"Nothing really, Anne. The mother is a nice woman and her son is going to play on my Little League team. He's a nice boy and needs a big brother to watch over him a bit, don't you think?"

"Yeah, yeah, he's a nice boy, but the mother is a nice girl, isn't she now, Mister Private Investigator? Do I detect an ulterior motive in your kindness?"

"Come on, Anne, Lorraine is a nice lady, but Gerald needs to make friends his own age. I think Little League will offer him that," said a smiling Jacob.

Anne walked out of Jacob's office with a smile the private eye could not see. There was turbulence ahead and a few curves, as they say in the baseball language. Good hitters have been known to send the ball over the center field fence when no one thought they could. Maybe Jacob was in for a bumpy ride.

Jacob started inspecting the three boxes filled with paper he had taken from Louis The Snake's place. The first one contained betting receipts, IOUs and notes about businessmen hooking up with whores from Louis' stable. Most of the names had a business telephone number with a letter at the end. Most likely some kind of code to identify the girl, the type of business or the guy himself. The second box contained similar papers plus two insurance policies, which he placed aside, and four different bankbooks. Two of the books, if they were current, showed large amounts of money. One had a balance as of three weeks ago of $89,000.86. The other was even higher, $145,000. Both bankbooks were in the name of Louis Billings. Now, he doubted Helen knew about these accounts or she would have said something about it. They showed deposits made on a regular monthly basis for amounts varying from 3 to 11K. The big surprise came in the third box where he found four different address books. Obviously, Louis liked to keep track of people he had dealings with. All the books had names of prominent people, local politicians, congressional representatives, senators, bank executives and many others. The red cover book was the one different from the others. Different in the sense that it contained names, addresses and telephone numbers of South American men, delegates from Arab embassies, African embassies and Eastern European countries. Each one had notes scribbled, indicating the number and type of guns they were looking for. Now here was a revelation Jacob thought would be most helpful to Lieutenant Jones or maybe even the FBI. No wonder Louis had so much money floating around in different bank accounts at different establishments. He called Anne and asked her to make copies of each page of this red book. "Keep in mind this is the most sensitive information we have ever handled. Make sure no one sees any of this material, Anne. I'll have another book for you after you're done with this first one."

Jacob was not sure in which direction this would take him. He knew from his friend Jones the mob was after him for something. They would not move too fast to get him because of his friendly relationship with the LAPD and the head of homicide, Lieutenant Bill Jones. The thought did occur to him that Tony Padilla might be after this one red book. It looked as if Louis was dealing weapons with foreign countries. He remembered Jones saying something about a series of weapons thefts from different military establishments nationwide. Therefore, Louis must have organized or even coordinated the group of thieves, or were they part of Padilla's national network? The latter made more sense. Louis must have been the contact man with the buyers. That also made sense. Money, large amounts of money in several bank accounts had to come from somewhere. Louis must have been skimming from the top and got caught. The Mafia does not mind if you steal, whatever it is that you steal, as long as it's not from them. That being the case, your number comes up quickly. In Louis' case, very quickly. It still did not answer why he, Jacob Schreiber, was being targeted.

When Anne came back, he had her copy all the bankbooks and the other address books. He asked her to place the contents securely in the office safe. Jacob picked up the telephone and dialed Helen Billings's number. After several rings a hungover sounding voice finally answered.

"Well, Jacob, did you find anything interesting on Cold Water Canyon the other day?" Helen asked.

"Not much except for a couple of insurance policies Louis had. One was a double indemnity on him in case of death by accident of some kind and the other was on your life. I'd like to bring them both to you today if I could, Helen, or would you prefer I gave them to your lawyer to handle?" Jacob said.

"You could do that, Harry will let me know what goes on."

After he was done talking with Helen, he looked at the important papers he had found and decided he should inform his friend from the LAPD. A fast telephone call would take care of it. "Lieutenant, this is Jacob. I have some good stuff here for you. You were on the right track when you talked about gun smuggling. Are you coming up my way today? I'll have it all packaged for you. Good, see you in a half hour or so." Jacob sorted out the important papers and address books only. He kept the bankbooks out of the package, because he felt they belonged to Helen. He didn't think Padilla was after the money, but was sure he would like to have those address books.

Anne had finished copying all the important papers and books. She placed the copied material in the wall safe and gave Jacob all the originals. Five different countries, twenty-two contact names with at least two telephone numbers to each. That alone was information worth a million dollars. Louis had taken months if not years to establish all the secured contacts. Furthermore, it appeared that payment for the shipment of stolen military weapons was well in place. Money was flowing regularly in four different accounts set up by Louis 'The Snake.' The more he thought about this, the more he felt the FBI should be involved.

There was a knock on the door and in came Bill Jones, all smiles and eager to see what this gumshoe had found. The lieutenant was as anxious as a teenager on his first date.

"Well, Jacob, what do you have for me to sink my teeth in?" Bill Jones asked. "I know it's going to be good stuff, but since you already know what you have, maybe you can give me an overall view of what I can expect."

"Lieutenant, after I'm done with showing you what's in this box here, you will have to call the FBI. This is heavy international stuff that probably, in political terms, threatens the national security. Louis and Padilla were dealing with international smugglers who buy arms for different dictatorships and pay cash. They don't care where the weapons come from as long as they are modern, up-to-date technology. Louis was definitely skimming off the top for years. Black Jack Tony didn't mind in the beginning because Louis was the one with the personal contacts. However, somewhere along the way it got very big and that's why I feel the FBI should be called in. Padilla and Billings were dealing stolen American weapons to foreign countries that could possibly use these same weapons against American troops. That is, without a doubt, for the Federal Bureau of Investigation to deal with. It's not important to me why Louis 'The Snake' was eliminated, but I would like to know why he was dumped on my office floor," Jacob concluded.

CHAPTER TEN...

Eight-thirty in the morning and the temperature was 75° with bright blue skies. Jacob was on his way to 988 Gregory in Beverly Hills. He had been told by a voice at the end of the intercom that Mr. Bill and Earl should be back home by yesterday. This time he parked near the gate entrance. He walked up to the pillar where the intercom system was and rang. A different voice answered, "May I ask who you are and what you are looking for?"

"You certainly may, my name is Jacob Schreiber and I would like to speak with Earl Edwards, please." There was a long buzz and as he pushed on the gate, it opened. Jacob was careful to quickly survey his surroundings to make sure there would not be any loose guard dogs coming at him. The driveway to the house was all bricks and wide enough for two cars. It took him a good three minutes to get to the front door where he rang again. This time the door opened and a tall slim man, balding a bit on top with grayish sideburns, welcomed Jacob.

"I'm Bill Watts, Mr. Schreiber. Earl will be here in a moment. Would you like to have a cup of coffee with us on the patio?" asked the man of the house.

"Given the time of day, that would be very nice, Mr. Watts. I understand you are a fashion designer for women and men's clothing," Jacob said.

The host kept walking towards an open doorway, obviously leading to the mentioned patio. When they got there, Jacob could not believe his eyes at the beauty of the gardens. In the middle of the whole thing was a fabulous Olympic sized swimming pool with diving board.

"Here comes Earl now, Mr. Schreiber. Should I leave you two alone?"

"Not at all, Mr. Watts, I only need to confirm something with Earl at his father's request."

"This is Mr. Schreiber, Earl. He wants to ask you something about your father, I think!"

"Hi! Earl, I'm Jacob Schreiber, a private investigator. Your father was a bit worried because he had not heard from you recently and asked me to try to find you. He mentioned a Board of Directors meeting you should be attending, next week if I am not mistaken. Do you have a problem with that?"

"Not at all," said the lanky well-tanned young man. "In fact, I did neglect to call my father because we were on a European trip and so busy the thought he would be worried never occurred to me. If you talk to him today, you can let him know I will be in Dallas next Tuesday on time for the Wednesday meeting. Is there anything else you had in mind to ask, Mr. Schreiber?"

Jacob thought for a moment, pulled out a business card which he dropped on the table and said gallantly, "Not really, Earl, as far as I'm concerned my mission is accomplished. I will call your father to let him know you are well and will be in Dallas next week. Thank you for the coffee, Mr. Watts, and if you are ever in need of a private investigator, I'll be happy to oblige."

"One never knows when the need will arise, Mr. Schreiber, but if I do, you will be the one I'll call on. Oh! Yes, I am an international designer."

Jacob got up and walked towards the house to return to the front gate where his old Packard was parked. On his way back to the office he thought about the surroundings he had just left. That's how he imagined rich people lived and that's what he had just seen. This Watts fellow must be extremely rich. They had walked by a garage big enough to store four cars, two of which he noticed were Italian models dating back to the late '20s. The house itself was really a mansion, so large with two stories, the whole thing sitting on two acres of land. Now he must call Leon Edwards and inform him his son has been found well-tanned and looking forward to arriving in Dallas next Tuesday.

When Jacob returned to his office, Anne was on the telephone talking in quite an animated way. He heard her say, "Just hold on Mrs. Billings, Mr. Schreiber just walked in."

Jacob motioned to his faithful secretary he would take the telephone in his office. "Well, Helen, what has made you so upset this morning?" he asked.

"I don't know who they were, certainly not the police, Jacob. Very rude people. They rang my doorbell and asked for you. I told them I knew you because you had investigated my husband for divorce purposes. The ugliest one of the two asked if you had either picked up papers from me or taken some to me. I told them, only because they were scary looking, you had taken Louis' paper inventory and given it to the police on my behalf, because it had to do with illegal gambling. Then they said they knew where your office is located and would get in touch with you. You know, Jacob, the more I think of it now, the more I feel these two guys were gangsters, they looked the part."

"Don't even have second thoughts, Helen; these individuals are after me, or I think they are. I may catch up to them later; thanks for letting me know." From the description Helen Billings had given him, Jacob was sure the two men were from Tony Padilla's gang of chess players. First he would talk to the Texas oilman then call the lieutenant. Things were going to get rough soon and he wanted to be prepared.

"Mr. Edwards, this is Jacob Schreiber in Hollywood. I have some good news for you. Yes, I located your son Earl and met with him. He told me he had been away to Europe on a long trip and then to San Francisco last week. He just returned to Beverly Hills yesterday. He will be taking an afternoon flight to Dallas next Tuesday, and said for you not to worry, he will be on time for the Board of Directors meeting." Jacob listened to the response from his client and then said, "The fee you left with me is much too much for what I did, Mr. Edwards. I would like to return part of it to you."

"There is no need for that, Mr. Schreiber, keep it as a retainer for future work I might ask you to do for me. Thanks again for responding immediately and for your straightforward honesty.

You're a good man to work with."

Jacob was pleased Edwards decided to leave all of the five grand as a retainer. *Who knows, I may have some more searching to do for him in the near future,* he thought.

"Lieutenant Jones, this is Jacob. I have some developments I would like to talk over with you. Yes, it's urgent. Padilla's goons were at Helen Billings's house today asking if I had taken any papers belonging to Louis. My feeling is they'll be coming to my office. If I'm here I can handle it, but I don't want my secretary to be hurt. These guys play for keeps and they don't care who they hurt or kill for that matter. Thanks, I look forward to seeing you; I'll have coffee ready."

He knew the lieutenant was on his side. There were other elements in the LAPD that could be worst than real gangsters. The only difference was the uniform they wore. Lieutenant William K. Jones was not one of them.

The telephone rang and he heard Anne telling the person to hold on for a moment.

"Jacob Schreiber, how can I help you?" he said.

"It's how you can help yourself, flatfoot. I'm only going to say this once, so listen very carefully. We are looking for a briefcase that belonged to Louis 'The Snake.' We know you have it because it's not at his house. In fact, one of my boys saw you go in Louis' wife's place empty handed and come out with a briefcase. We want that briefcase and what's in it. Tomorrow morning by ten I'll have one of my boys pick it up from your office. If what I am looking for is in it, you'll get an envelope with a grand in it. If on the other hand it's not... you're a dead duck, shamus."

Before Jacob could say anything, the man had hung up. *Nice person*, he thought, *I better have my reception committee here when this joker shows up in the morning.*

"Anne, I would like you to take the morning off tomorrow. I'm going to have some nasty company here and you don't need to be exposed to their terrible behavior."

"Are you sure you'll be okay, Jacob?" As she was going to say

THE BOOKIE

more, a knock on the door distracted her. She turned around to see the smiling face of Detective Jones.

"May I come in, or should I wait in the reception area?" said a jesting police officer.

"Come on in, Bill; Anne was just walking away as you knocked. I do have some important matters to talk over with you. Here's a fresh cup of coffee for you. I just got a call from some goon threatening me if I don't turn over a briefcase he thinks I have that used to belong to our friend Louis. As a matter of fact, I do have it." Jacob reached under his desk and pulled an old style flat briefcase with a center lock on it. "I don't have the key, but let's see how hard it is to open." He opened his desk drawer, pulled a twelve-inch flat screwdriver and with one flip of the wrist, the lock broke off. Inside were several pieces of paper known as markers in Louis' bookie days, two notebooks, several photographs of "lightly dressed" ladies, an old bank book and a key which looked like it could be a locker style key or a bank deposit key. There was also a small rolled up piece of paper with elastic around it, a few pencils and an old bankbook. Jacob handed the notebooks to the lieutenant while he took time to check the bankbook. This one was an updated version of what he had found at the house. The balance showing was $250,000. He wondered for a moment if the money was really in the bank. "Well, what do you think, Lieutenant? Anything interesting in those two books?"

"There sure is, Jacob. Would you believe that he has in here a list of prominent business people and politicians with telephone numbers and some kind of code at the end of each one with a letter that certainly meant something to Louis. I noticed that he only uses the letters N, B, F and W. We should be able to break the code easily, it looks so damn simple. Did you find anything interesting in the bankbook?"

"This book seems to be a savings account with a quarter of a million posted in it. Helen Billings is a rich widow if she can stay alive and sober long enough to enjoy it all. The box I gave you yesterday, did you have a chance to go through it yet?"

"I did, Jacob, and I had a meeting with Paul Trickten, an FBI special agent here in Los Angeles. We spent three hours together going through the information in the books. He was quite pleased. I told him you were the one who got the papers. Special agent Trickten said he would contact you in a few days. He did tell me though, the Padilla gang was suspected of arms trafficking and they had several agents assigned to watch them. Maybe with this evidence they could now proceed with arrest warrants. You said on the telephone you had received a threat from someone you suspect belongs to the Padilla's stable. Did you want to elaborate a bit more on that?"

"I guess they picked on me thinking Louis had left something behind for me to hold. They're right on that, but it was all post mortem, if I may say. I would like to prepare a little surprise for whoever is coming here in the morning. For that, I need your help, Lieutenant. I already told Anne to take the morning off. No need for her to witness any rough stuff or get hurt for that matter. Would you be willing to participate?"

The lieutenant said, "My brother had warned me about you. I didn't know what he meant at the time when he said you were addictive. I'm beginning to find out. Let's hear what you have in mind, my friend."

CHAPTER ELEVEN...

The scenario was simple. At the reception desk, a young rookie police officer whom Lieutenant Jones had under his wings. Sitting in the two waiting room chairs were two seasoned detectives and in Jacob's office, Jones and the gumshoe. At the entrance of the building, a plain-clothes officer was also posted to keep an eye on people walking in. This officer also kept an eye on who parked near the curb, close to the entrance. At the top of the stairs, another detective in case someone would take the elevator to a higher floor and then use the fire stairwell to come down. This whole plan had been thought out by Jacob, but executed by the lieutenant. They wanted to be sure that whoever was coming to get the briefcase would be arrested before he had a chance to do any real damage.

The ringing of the telephone startled everyone. Jacob picked it up himself. "This is Jacob Schreiber, how can I help you?"

"Well, flatfoot," said the gruff voice, "I see you're in early. My man is on his way to see you. Remember what I said yesterday, you either have what I want and give it to me and live, or you're a dead duck."

Again, just as it had happened yesterday, before Jacob could say anything, the man hung up. "Same voice, Lieutenant, says his man is on the way here. Better tell your guys to be on the lookout."

Lieutenant Jones left the office for a quick walk down the hall and downstairs. He saw that all his men were at their proper posts, awaiting orders. As he reached the lobby, he had a view of the street outside. Cars coming and going. Then a black Cadillac with heavily tinted windows pulled close to the sidewalk in the non-parking zone. The rear door opened and the detective saw a heavyset man walking out towards the building entrance. He also noticed another man sitting in the back. Now was time for action. On his signal four officers went to the car, opened the front and rear doors, and with guns drawn, they motioned everyone inside to come out. Three men came out with their hands up in the air. They were frisked and four weapons were confiscated. All were then handcuffed and each one placed in the back of an unidentified patrol car. The guy who had been sitting in the back seat of the Cadillac was Tony Padilla, the so-called 'godfather' of the California Mafia. He (Padilla) was making all kinds of noises, threats like, "Don't you guys know who I am?" as if the officers cared. One pulled out a roll of heavy tape and sealed his mouth. Now that would not place this officer in the good graces of Mr. Padilla. They pushed him on the back seat of a patrol car with the windows up and locked the doors. One officer remarked that he had wanted to do this to the scumbag for a long time. Without his goons around, he was nothing and they intended to keep him that way for a while.

When the courier arrived at Jacob's office door, he did not even have the politeness to knock. Just barged in and when he saw there were two men sitting there, he just asked if the gumshoe was in.

The officer playing the secretary said, "You will have to wait your turn, sir, and whom should I say wants to see Mr. Schreiber?"

"Tell him it's the undertaker and I don't have time to wait with these clowns here," said the burley, scruffy individual. He made a move towards Jacob's closed office door and as he did, the two officers who had been sitting quietly along with the receptionist sprang onto the man. They had him handcuffed in a moment and removed two firearms as well as a dagger from him.

"Nice guy you are, I bet you didn't serve time in the army," said one officer.

"He sure doesn't know how to obey orders, does he now? We ought to make sure he understands English properly before we throw him down the stairs," said the second officer.

Jacob came out of his office with a grin on his face. "Do you have a name or do I just call you asshole?" The scruffy guy didn't bother answering Jacob. "Officer, why don't you check if the man has a wallet," Jacob said. "That way we won't have to fingerprint him immediately."

THE BOOKIE

"Here it is," said the officer who searched the man. "What do you know, he doesn't have a local driver's license. This is from New Jersey and it says his name is Lorenzo Spamonte. It even has his ugly face on it. You know carrying dangerous weapons from another state is a federal offence if my memory serves me right, Mr. Schreiber. Maybe we should call in the FBI and turn this guy over to them. It'll save our taxpayers money. I wonder how his friends are doing downstairs?"

As he was finishing his words, the lieutenant walked in with the news they had arrested Tony Padilla and two goons who had unlicensed firearms on them. "Did you have a hard time with this pretty boy?" he asked as he looked towards the handcuffed guy. "Well, we are done here for the day unless Mister... what's your name?" he asked.

Spamonte just cursed at the lieutenant. One officer close by let him have a hard left jab to the middle, which made him grunt and bend forward. "It's not nice to swear at my boss, you know," said the officer.

The three officers escorted Padilla's gofer out of Jacob's office. Lieutenant Jones looked at his watch and said, "Not even nine-thirty and the laundry is already washed. Not bad for an early morning workout. Would you not say so, Jacob?"

"On a scale of one to ten, this has to be a 9 3/4. What remains to be seen is what Tony will or won't do now. Do you think he got the message that you and I sometimes work together?"

"Well, Jacob, if he didn't, he soon will. The FBI is waiting at my headquarters to pick him up. Our Mr. Padilla has some long days, if not weeks, ahead of him. I was informed they had enough to charge him with weapons trafficking, which will prevent him from getting bail this time. This type of federal offence is considered on the same level as national security. He will not be bothering you for some time, Jacob. It could take four to five years or more before the case goes to court. Someone will be looking at taking over Tony's business in a very short time. We are looking at some rough times ahead of us in the coming weeks. Once the dust settles down and everyone realizes

Tony is not coming back any time soon, infighting will begin. There will be a few dead bodies around. Such is life, my friend. Don't give up your guard, we have not closed the file on Louis the bookie yet."

The lieutenant left to join his men on their way to police headquarters.

Jacob was happy to see things had gone smoothly. He sat at his desk to enjoy a coffee and doughnut. The telephone ring startled him. "Jacob is the name, investigation is the game. Schreiber here."

"My oh my, you are in a playful mood, Mr. Schreiber. Something real good must have happened today. This is Lorraine Buford. Just wanted to let you know Gerald and I will be at the practice tomorrow. He's really looking forward to seeing you again and meeting some kids his age. You have made quite an impression on this little boy. While I have a chance I want to thank you for what you did for us."

"Well, Miss Buford, I was hoping to make an impression on the mother too. It's nice to hear from you and I'm looking forward to seeing you both tomorrow. If you have time, we could go for hamburgers after the practice. The treat is on me, what do you say?"

"Best offer I had today, Mr. Schreiber, and do you think you could call me Lorraine? I would feel so much better, if not younger."

"Not a problem, Lorraine, and the name is Jacob. Look forward to seeing you both at the park tomorrow."

Jacob could not believe what he had just said. He liked young Gerald and felt sorry for him, having lost his dad in the war. More importantly, he had strong feelings towards Lorraine Buford. She was a pretty woman, tall and approximately two to three years younger than he was. Who knows where this would go and what will happen were his thoughts when the telephone rang again to take him out of his daydreaming. "Jacob Schreiber here, how can I help you?" "This is Special Agent Paul Trickten of the FBI, Mr. Schreiber. Your friend Lieutenant Jones of the LAPD brought me up to date on what you had found in Louis Billings' briefcase. Would you have some time to talk with me today?"

"For the FBI and to rid our society of the likes of Padilla, I'm available to you at any time. Sure, early afternoon is fine with me, see you then, Mr. Trickten." *For once, they are moving fast,* thought Jacob. The thefts of military weapons from different installations across the nation must be a big concern to the FBI and the military authorities too. Jacob went to his wall safe and took out the papers he had copied and brought them to his desk. Maybe he missed something. He placed the bankbooks in his middle drawer. The gumshoe had wanted to turn them over to Helen's lawyer for verification but had not done so yet. He heard the door open and got up to investigate.

"Well, Mr. Detective, how was the rough stuff this morning?" Anne asked. "My time off allowed me to shop for my visitors. It doesn't look as if there was much of a scuffle in here, does it now?"

"No, Anne, the scuffle was very brief with three police officers to handle it. I enjoyed watching it. Maybe I can have some quiet time and concentrate on real work for a change. So that you know, I'm expecting an FBI agent shortly. His name is Paul Trickten. I'm going to grab a sandwich downstairs. I should be back in twenty minutes or so," Jacob concluded.

When Jacob returned to the office, Trickten had not arrived yet. He went through the papers once more to make certain he had not missed anything of importance. Then he saw that little piece of paper with a rubber band tied around it. He picked it up, took the rubber band away, and unfolded the small paper to see the name of a banking institution hand-printed on it. The address was in Beverly Hills. Also printed on the paper were a series of five consecutive numbers and a hyphen followed by a two-digit number. Inside the paper was the key, which had fallen out of the briefcase. He picked it up and stared at it. At first, he couldn't see the numbers on it because they were too small. He opened his side drawer and picked up a magnifying glass. "Bingo," he exclaimed. "That key is for a safety deposit box at a Beverly Hills Home Savings branch." He just sat there wondering what secrets this safety deposit box could hold. Louis 'The Snake' had many things going, but unfortunately for him, they were all bad. *Being a bookie is not a job, it's a hazard,* Jacob thought. It's almost like walking through a minefield without a Geiger counter. He placed the key and paper in his wallet. He would have to make time to investigate this bank safety deposit box. *Noon is usually a good time*, he thought. Head bankers are gone to lunch and new employees are just there holding the place open, telling people who wanted to see the manager or bank president they would have to come back after lunch. He figured his chances of being able to pass himself as Louis were better with a young inexperienced employee. Tomorrow would be the perfect day.

There was a knock on his door and Anne said, "Mr. Trickten of the FBI is here to see you, Jacob."

"Bring him in, Anne. Good afternoon, sir, please have a seat."

"Thank you, Mr. Schreiber," said the special agent. "I gather you know why I am here. The papers you found and turned over to Lieutenant Jones have enabled us to almost complete our investigation into the illegal arms trafficking operation of Tony Padilla and the late Louis Billings. There are still some loose ends to gather and I have a feeling you'll be able to help us," Trickten concluded.

"I certainly hope I can do that. Padilla and his goons need to be put away for a long time. Not only do they steal weapons from our military to resell to countries that could eventually use them against us, but the drug trade they operate has to be slowed down, if not eliminated," Jacob said.

"Let me show you some other papers I have found," the gumshoe said with a smile.

CHAPTER TWELVE...

When Jacob arrived at the branch of Home Savings in Beverly Hills, it was just past noon. He thought this would be the best time when no one would bother to ask for IDs. He was right. When he showed his key, the young bank clerk looked at the number on it and immediately took Jacob to the vault. Once there, he asked Jacob for his key, and placed it in the slot below the key of the bank. He handed Jacob a big metal drawer and showed him the area where he could have privacy. Once alone in the secured area, he took the lid off the drawer. Stocks, bonds, another copy of a life insurance policy and a little black book. Fifteen tightly wrapped hundred dollar bills in bundles of 50. A cool $75,000. This was part of the skimming Louis had been doing for years. Hidden money for a rainy day or a fast getaway. Jacob had carried an empty briefcase with him. He placed everything in it and would check it out in the privacy of his office. He opened the door of the cubicle and motioned to the young man that he was finished. He got the key back and left the bank before anyone could ask him who he was. It had been too easy for him to get to Louis Billings' confidential papers. Helen Billings had been a big help. She really did not want to know about her deceased husband's crooked deals. One thing he was going to do was turn over the found bankbooks to Helen's attorney along with the stocks and bonds he had located. No need to tell the attorney where he got them, just turn them over instead of giving them to the police. For the time being, he would place the found cash in his office safe with his secretary's knowledge. The black book, after copying it, he would turn over to the FBI.

"Well, Anne, you look surprised to see me, anything wrong?" he asked.

"No, Jacob, nothing's wrong. I was not expecting you until later, before you leave for Griffith Park to go play with the kids. I have three calls here for you to return. Possibly a new client or two. And this one you don't have to return. Gerald Buford wanted to know if you are going to be there for sure. I told him you wouldn't miss it for the world, especially since his mother is going to be with him," she concluded with a smile on her face.

"Now, now, Anne, do I detect a bit of sarcasm here?"

"Not at all, Jacob. I think she's a nice woman and her boy is a well brought up kid. It's just that I noticed how you talked to her. You know what I mean, not in the same tone you would talk with a client. My husband and I have been saying for some time you should find a nice woman and build yourself a relationship. Do you find anything wrong with that, Jacob?"

"I really don't, but please don't play cupid with me. I'm old enough to trap myself without guidance. While I'm here," as he dumped the stacks of money on her desk, "could you place this cash in our secured safe? So that you know, I stole it from the bank an hour ago. The cops are not here yet! You don't even look surprised. There's seventy-five grand in there and it belonged to Louis 'The Snake.' I got it from a safety deposit box at the branch of Home Savings in Beverly Hills. For the time being, only you and I are to know about this money and where it came from. I have to see how things develop before I funnel it in one direction or the other. Would you do me the favor and call Special Agent Trickten right away? I need to have a quick talk with him. If he's not there, leave an urgent message. Could you also copy this black book, every page that has something written on? Oh yes, I'll be going to the park in about an hour," Jacob concluded with a smile on his face.

"Agent Trickten, Jacob Schreiber here. I have something new I found amongst my stack of papers today. It's a little black book, if I may call it that. It contains names, telephone numbers, dates of transactions, where the weapons were stolen and by whom, and how these weapons were brought to a warehouse here in Los Angeles owned by a Mr. Anthony Padilla. It tells how the weapons were packed for shipment and the method used to prevent customs from verifying the contents. It shows bribes paid to officials, names of the officials and where they work. By any chance would you be interested in this book?" Jacob went on to say that he would be leaving the office shortly but his secretary should be here until 4 PM if he could come by. "Good, I'll have it in an envelope for you, and let's get together for coffee later this week if you can."

In building new relationships with police agencies, Jacob had his sights on the future. He knew that by cooperating with the LAPD he was able to strike a valuable friendship with Lieutenant Bill Jones. If he could do the same with Special Agent Paul Trickten, he felt it could be beneficial to both sides. In many of his investigations, it came in handy to work with the authorities instead of having to work against them. Case in point, Louis Billings and his shady operation as a bookie. At times it also provided Jacob with answers that could have taken as long as a week, if not a month to get.

He looked over all the papers he had dumped on his desk and felt reassured he had not forgotten any possible lead which could help both the LAPD and the FBI. He placed them all back in the two large envelopes provided and returned them to the safe. He knew Louis had been snuffed out on an order from Tony Padilla, so did the cops, but proving it would be an almost impossible task. *Unless*, he thought, *a definite motive could be established.* Money had been Jacob's early reasoning. With all this new information on the operation of the illegal gun sales, a fresh and stronger motive was surfacing. He placed all the thoughts back to memory and prepared himself for Little League practice. On his way out, he gave Anne the book Special Agent Trickten was going to pick up shortly.

"I'm going to play ball with the kids for the next two hours. If you have anything needing my attention, leave a message on my desk, I'll stop by on my way home."

"Don't forget to call those two names I gave you; Joan Libbit seemed anxious to talk with you. She said it was about a possible divorce. Her husband owns a large trucking company. Oh yeah, have a good time at the park," Anne said with a big smile on her face.

Jacob left the office with a spring in his walk. For some reason, he felt better than usual. Could it be that meeting Lorraine Buford was having an effect on him? He was ready to play it smart. Let the chips fall where they may, as the saying goes. For some reason, this sounded like what a gambler at a dice table would say. When he got to the parking lot, he noticed many kids were there. Some with parents, others not. He opened the trunk of his car, took out a bag full of baseballs, a half dozen bats, a catcher's mitt, a first baseman's glove and a couple of spare gloves for kids who may have forgotten theirs or did not have one. As he walked in the direction of one of the backstops, four or five kids came screaming at him, happy to see their coach. Then he saw Lorraine and Gerald. He motioned them to come over.

"Hey, guys, this is Gerald Buford. His father was in the Marines with me during the war. More importantly, Gerald is a short stop with a strong arm. Let's welcome him to the team." From the corner of his eyes, he saw Gerald immediately mix with the other kids. Lorraine was standing back with a smile on her face.

"I'm going to ask you, Lorraine, to keep an eye on the equipment. We've had some missing in previous years. I hope you don't mind doing that. My attention will be with the kids for the next hour."

"I'm very happy to do it, Jacob. Seeing my son come out of his shell and be happy is very important to me. Oh, by the way, we are free to go for hamburgers after the practice," Lorraine said. Jacob just smiled back.

She just sat there and watched Jacob talk with the children, giving them instructions on how to catch a rolling ball, then a fly ball. He seemed to have an extra reserve of patience when it came to these young boys. He got them to throw, to pitch, to catch and to bat the ball too. She barely understood what baseball was all about but was willing to learn, if not for her son, at least for Jacob.

When the practice was over Jacob got all the kids and parents together for a final pep talk until next week. He invited everyone for drinks (coke or seven-up) and hot dogs at Charlie's on Hollywood Boulevard near Van Ness.

"If you can make it, the treat's on me," said the happy gumshoe. There was a big cheer from the whole group and everyone proceeded to their separate transportation.

"Lorraine, do you know where this place is? You could always follow me if you don't," Jacob said.

"Are you sure you can do this, Jacob?"

"I never make an invitation I can't follow up on. Besides, I saw the sparkle in Gerald's face and that was enough for me. I see he's already made a couple of friends. That's great, don't you think, Lorraine?"

"I don't know what to say, Jacob. I feel as if I'm in a dream and don't want to wake up. I certainly hope it keeps on going. I never had so much fun watching kids play ball in my whole life. Thank you, Jacob."

"Don't say that, Lorraine, you're embarrassing me. Playing with these innocent children makes me forget how nasty the real world is out there. I would not change it for anything. Money cannot buy this feeling, knowing that for whatever short period of time, once a week, I can make these children happy. This is not a chore. To me this is relaxation. Here comes Gerald, better get to your car. I'll see you at Charlie's."

After everyone had gone home, there was only Lorraine, Gerald and Jacob left behind. "So, Gerald, do you think you'd like to be on my team?" Jacob asked an excited boy.

"I sure want to, Mr. Schreiber. I made a couple of friends tonight. One lives a couple of blocks from where we live. It's kind of neat, yeah, I really want to play ball with this gang."

Looking at the mother, Jacob said, "Did you bring the registration paper with you, Lorraine? Thanks, I'll turn it in to the league secretary tomorrow. Next week, same time, same place, we'll have another practice, then the following Saturday is the first get-together of the year where all the kids from every team in the league and their parents will be there. Hot dogs, games and whatever. It's a fun afternoon for everyone. A time for the kids to get to know everyone they will be playing with. You don't want to miss this," Jacob concluded.

"We won't miss this for anything, Jacob. Do you think I could invite you to have dinner with us the day after tomorrow, if you're not busy that is?" said a happy faced lady.

"I don't remember anything scheduled two days down the road. Best invitation I've had this week," Jacob said, tongue in cheek.

Jacob waited to make sure they were both safely in their car and on the way home. He felt a sense of accomplishment and a tingling inside himself he had not felt before.

CHAPTER THIRTEEN...

Paul Trickten was quite happy that Jacob Schreiber was the one who had found the papers, notes and little black books from Louis Billings' collection of memorabilia. If anyone else but the shrewd private detective and former Marine had found them, Trickten was convinced he would have never seen the content. *Schreiber*, he thought, *displayed honesty and a willingness to cooperate, something rare amongst the gumshoe society.* Today would be a good day to have coffee and doughnuts with someone he was beginning to appreciate. Paul picked the telephone and dialed Schreiber's number. "Is Mr. Schreiber in please? This is Special Agent Paul Trickten of the FBI. Thank you, I'll wait.

"Good morning Jacob, do you have time to meet me for coffee and some gossip this morning?" said a cheerful FBI agent.

"I do, Paul, and where would you like to meet? Does the Santa Monica Pier sound okay to you? We'll have lots of privacy there and fresh air at the same time. Good, I'll see you in about forty-five minutes." Jacob wondered what the G-man had in mind. He probably wanted to talk about the findings in all the black books and notes from Louis' junk pile. That was the obvious, now what could be out of the ordinary? *FBI men are not usually that friendly*, Jacob thought. Maybe this guy was different. He had everything to gain by building a friendship with Trickten.

Anne walking into the office took him away from his thinking time. "What do you have in mind, may I ask?" Jacob said.

"Nothing special, Jacob, just wanted to know how the practice went the other night. You never talked about it. Did something go wrong?" asked a very curious secretary.

"What you're trying to say, Anne, is more like: did you have a good time with Lorraine Buford, or did you take her out after you dumped the kid, or—"

"No, no, Jacob, I was really wondering if her son did well at the practice and joined your team. Of course I want to know about her and you, that's only natural, don't you think? A little gossip never hurts."

"The practice was great. Gerald made friends immediately. After the game was over, I took all the kids and their parents, those who were there, to Charlie's for cokes and hot dogs. The mother was elated and she invited me to dinner on Friday." Laughing loudly Jacob told Anne, "Had you going for a moment, didn't I? Don't push, Anne, I told you earlier I was mature enough to make my own mistakes. Although I don't think I'm making one now. Lorraine is a nice woman and her son needed to get to know kids his age. I don't think it's too easy for a war widow to bring up a son. The male image not being there for the boy could possibly cause some discipline problems. In the case of Gerald, it seems he has adjusted well so far. At practice, he was quick at making friends with everyone. That's always a good sign when you see a kid who can relate with others his own age. Now, my dear secretary, are you satisfied with the social report?" asked a smiling private eye. "I have to get going now. I'm meeting with Paul Trickten for coffee at the Santa Monica Pier. I should be back here in about two hours."

"You go ahead, Mr. Detective, and thanks for filling me in on your social activities. Hope your Friday dinner goes well too. Don't forget to bring flowers and wine." Anne had been working with Jacob from the day he first opened his office. When her husband first met Jacob, they got along right from the beginning. They had become almost like brothers toward one another. Jack taught law at UCLA. Criminology was his bag. So when the two got together, conversation topics were never scarce.

The ringing of the telephone made her jump slightly. "Jacob Schreiber Investigations, how can I help you? This is Anne."

"Oh hi, Anne, Lucy here from the DA's office, is Jacob in?"

"He just left for Santa Monica, should be back before noon. Can I have him call you back or would you prefer to leave a message?"

"Could you tell him that the ME and the DA are having a meeting early afternoon, say around two, and would like to see Mr. Schreiber."

"Not a problem, Lucy. I'll let him know, talk to you soon."

Now I wonder what these two guys have up their sleeves. Too many bodies falling close to my boss, I guess. The medical examiner would certainly have a bunch of questions regarding the notes with Jacob's name left in the pockets of David Ross and Louis Billings too. I suppose the DA is concerned with public opinion where a licensed private investigator who should uphold the law at all times suddenly finds himself the depository of murdered people. I don't think the DA realizes the danger Jacob places himself in when investigating people of doubtful reputation. Anne was just in a thinking mood. She also wondered if he had called this Joan Libbit back. *Maybe he'll let me know when he returns from his meeting with the FBI.*

At the Santa Monica Pier, Jacob parked in his usual spot, walked to the entrance of the pier and spotted Trickten looking over the railing. He approached him quietly. The man didn't even turn his head.

"Beautiful morning to let your thoughts float on the ocean, Paul," Jacob said.

"Good morning, Jacob. At this time of day the peaceful surroundings of the pier added to the noise of the breaking waves just takes your mind off the daily tribulations of work. I should come here more often, it's good for the soul, don't you think?"

Jacob said, "When I want to clear the cobwebs, I come here for a long walk and a hotdog. This place seems to invite your thoughts to flow out of your head and ride the waves. Let's go get a coffee and doughnut, then you can tell me what's on your mind."

Paul had dropped the tie and jacket for the walk on the pier. He certainly didn't want to look too official. Once they got their morning java, they headed towards the end of the pier where no one was at this early hour. Tourists would swamp this place later in the day. Locals who came here to fish off the dock, which did not require a license, only showed up when the tide was up. Fishing was better at high tide.

Jacob began the conversation. "Did you want to talk about the findings I handed over to you, Paul, or is it something else?"

Paul replied, "I'm concerned about the motivation behind the killings of Billings and Terry Downs. It appears money-related, which it partly is, but the fact that one body was dumped in your office and the other had a paper in his pocket with your name and telephone number bothers me. Neither of those people were clients of yours. From my analysis, I feel someone within Padilla's group, or even Padilla himself, has a bone to pick with you. Did you ever kill any of Padilla's relatives?" asked the FBI operative.

Jacob answered, "No, I'm sure that is not the case. I remember a few months ago testifying at the trial of Luciano Padilla, Tony's younger brother, who was facing a murder charge for killing a liquor store clerk during a robbery in West Los Angeles. It was pure coincidence. I was going in the store to buy a bottle of wine. As I got out of my car, I heard a gun shot. Instinct made me pull my own gun out and lucky I did. Anyway, I shot the guy in the shoulder and held him there until the ambulance and cops arrived. At the trial, I identified Luciano as the young man running out of the store with a gun in his hands. Later, when Padilla was awaiting transfer, he was stabbed to death in the exercise yard of the pen, so I was informed. I never gave it a second thought, but it could be that Tony Padilla blames me for his younger brother's death. Look at it this way, Paul, I do think Louis 'The Snake' crossed his wires somewhere along the line. Maybe Padilla figured Louis knew too much and it was time to get rid of him permanently. Terry Downs and David Ross were two bookies who worked in cooperation with Billings. It's possible David Ross was observed coming to my office and you know what a mafioso thinks about talking to cops or private eyes. As far as they are concerned, I'm no better than a cop is and since I don't have the big machinery behind me, I'm an easier target. I wish I had had a chance to talk with Ross. I do think they began to panic a bit when a soldier was killed at a military depot during an attempted robbery. Unless you have something different in mind, that's the best I can come up with."

"Well," Paul said, "I was curious as to how you got all this information, papers, books, etc. It seems to me someone must have turned it over to you, unless you're hiding something from us. Which is it, Jacob?"

"I can understand your apprehensions, Paul. Helen Billings was a client of mine. I did some work for her, which she could have used in her upcoming divorce with Louis. They had been separated for almost two years, but were still on a somewhat friendly basis, if you can believe that. She gave me the briefcase containing all the books and papers on the weapons operation. Helen did not know what was in the briefcase nor did she want to. There was an amount of money, which I gave back to her. She also gave me the keys to Louis' house and told me there were more papers in shoe boxes stashed away in a closet. That's how I came across this big mess. I gave a bunch to Lieutenant Jones and suggested he turn whatever was not related to the murder case to the FBI. Once he had done that and informed you about the source, you know the rest of it. Now, the evidence in regards to the weapons thefts should be strong enough to put Padilla away for a long time, don't you think?"

Paul said, "We are going to arrest Tony Padilla and several of his henchmen officially today. They have been in the LAPD custody for a few days and will be turned over to us this afternoon. As we speak, the Attorney General is in front of a federal court judge, laying out the groundwork. At one point, we are going to need your testimony as to the origin of these documents. I'm sure our attorneys will let you know when you're needed. I just want you to know, Jacob, that your cooperation has been a great help to me. It has saved us months, if not years, of work trying to pin down Padilla and his associates nationwide. If at any time you require my help, I want you to feel free to call on me. What's the old saying? 'I owe you one.'"

The two of them left the Santa Monica Pier happy to have begun a friendly association, if not a real friendship.

On his way back Jacob thought the G-man was not such a bad guy after all. His father had always told him to be careful, but to keep an open mind. A friendship can develop unexpectedly. These friendships usually lasted a lifetime. How wise his father had been. Too bad he was not around to share with him now. Oh well, there was always Anne at the office. He knew she could be trusted with anything he had to say and give him a truthful opinion in return.

The first thing Anne said when he walked in was, "Jacob, did you call Joan Libbit? Also, Lucy from the DA's office wants you to call back. Apparently, the ME and the DA want to see you at a meeting around two this afternoon. How was your meeting with the FBI? Are they going to throw the book at you yet?"

Jacob answered, "Would you believe I'm going to be sent to a federal pen later? Trickten said they had enough on me to lock me up for ten years."

"I know you're just kidding, but please call Mrs. Libbit, and don't forget Lucy at the DA's office too."

CHAPTER FOURTEEN...

Joan Libbit was not happy with her husband's adventures. As a child growing up in a small village in the Midwest, there were strict rules to follow. First the obedience at home and at school. Attending services at the Catholic Church was part of the weekly routine she had to follow. In the beginning, she believed marriage to be the length of one's life. How your priorities change as you get older, she was telling Jacob.

"You know, Mr. Schreiber, the first ten years were wonderful. I don't think he cheated on me at that time. Once a woman becomes a mother five times over, her youthful figure disappears fast. Because of all the work and caring to be done for the children, the husband is sometimes neglected. Still, that should not allow him to go around with prostitutes and other women. I was not able to do that, go around with other men that is. He did not fulfill his contract to me and I want him to pay for it. I need for you to find some concrete proof." Joan Libbit placed an unsealed envelope on Jacob's desk "This is a $3,000 retainer for you to begin. My husband Larry owns a fleet of trucks that transports cargo nationwide. He has some exclusive contracts that are very lucrative. His financial report from last year, here's a copy of it, shows a profit after taxes of three million dollars. I listed a number of bars he likes to hang around and a couple of photographs to help you identify him."

"Thank you, Mrs. Libbit, I'll get working on this right away. The moment I have some information you'll hear from me," Jacob concluded.

After Joan Libbit left his office, Jacob directed his thoughts on Tony Padilla and his younger brother Luciano. The more he thought about it, the more he came to the conclusion Padilla wanted to cause him problems with the authorities. Possibly have his license suspended or even revoked. So far it had not worked, but why him?

Tony could have easily put a contract on Jacob, he didn't do that. The man did not want to kill him. There had to be a different motivating factor behind all this. The motive wasn't important at this time since Padilla and six of his goons were in federal hands.

He heard the telephone ring and Anne answered it in her usual professional way.

"It's for you, Jacob, Lieutenant Jones is on the line," Anne said.

"What brings you to my world, Lieutenant? No more bodies with my card in their pockets, I hope. Even the FBI thinks I have a special magnet that attracts all bad elements towards me."

"I am not prepared to say all, Jacob, but a few... yes. Just got a call from Paul Trickten. Padilla and his associates have been charged with theft of military weapons for the purpose of illegal trafficking to third world nations. This charge in itself is a breach of national security that could carry life imprisonment or, if treason is added, death. They are also charged with possession of cocaine for the purpose of trafficking and Padilla has an additional charge of murder for the killing of Louis Billings. The FBI searched Mr. Padilla's residence in the Palisades. Would you believe cocaine, heroin and marijuana were found in a well-hidden concrete basement? Paul also told me more evidence of the arms dealings was found. Be prepared, Jacob, our Mr. Padilla is not going anywhere but a federal pen for life. If the murder conviction doesn't stick, the drug charges carry a life sentence too. There will be war in the trenches to see who takes over big Tony's place in our friendly world of undesirables," Lieutenant Jones concluded.

"Wow!" said Jacob. "That will fix his rap sheet for some time. Don't you think they are too optimistic about pinning Tony Padilla with Billings' murder? That is still a local issue the DA will have to deal with. Talking about the devil... I received an invitation to Fundalee's office to meet with him and the ME this afternoon. I guess they didn't want to buy me lunch, so the meeting was set for 2 o'clock. Wouldn't you like to drop in, Lieutenant?"

"It sounds interesting, but I have some other avenues to check today. There were three other murders in my jurisdiction last night.

I'm short of personnel and the workload is increasing. Just wanted you to know some of the information that will not be made public for a few days, if not weeks. Let's keep in touch on any new development," concluded the detective.

Jacob returned to his thoughts on the motivation for Louis Billings' murder. *Could it be that Padilla thought Louis was going to spill the beans on their weapons operation? On the other hand, could it be that Louis threatened them to do exactly that by telling them he had given me the information for safe keeping? So many possibilities and no way to explore them openly since Louis is no longer amongst the living.* There was still the question of the seventy-five grand sitting in his safe and what to do with it. He decided to wait for a while. He had already turned over several bankbooks along with the loose cash totaling almost two million dollars. Helen Billings and her lawyer were handling that part of it. No one was aware of the safety deposit box in a Beverly Hills branch of Home Savings and Loan. All papers found in there were given to the FBI, only the cash he had kept aside. The money, he had already figured, had been skimmed from dealings with Padilla. A slush fund for doing 'pro bono' cases suddenly occurred to him. There were always people referred to him by friends, lawyers he knew and even judges who trusted his integrity when it came to dealing with human behavior. People who needed the help of an investigator, but could not afford the cost. In his short time as a PI, Jacob had built a reputation for honesty and fairness. He was known for quick action and fast results. A nononsense investigator who was not afraid to tell it as he saw it. That reputation was helping him when he dealt directly with law enforcement agencies or high-ticket attorneys. It made it easier for him to get needed information without having to go through the regular red tape. *Now,* he thought, *a slush fund of that magnitude would go a long way to help those who would otherwise suffer the injustices of a mean society.*

He was so deep in thought that Anne had to knock real hard on his door to remind him of his 2 o'clock meeting at the DA's office. "Is it that time already?" said a startled Jacob. "Thanks for reminding me,

Anne. By the way, what kind of flowers should I bring to my dinner host on Friday? You think roses would be appropriate, or should I have a mix combination; what do you say?"

Anne replied, "I think roses are always welcome. Don't forget to bring a small thing for the boy."

"Like a baseball or some baseball cards? I don't want to go overboard on the first dinner invitation, you know. I don't want them to think I'm cheap either. Know what I mean, Anne? Since the boy is going to play on my team, I must be careful not to show too much favoritism toward him. The other kids will shy away from Gerald, and that won't be good. I have to think this over well," Jacob concluded as he departed for his first meeting with the DA in a long time.

When he got to the DA's office, Lucy immediately showed him in. Jack Fundalee introduced Jacob to his new assistant Robert Armstrong.

The DA said, "We're still waiting for Doctor Stitch to show up, Jacob. He sometimes gets delayed at the bar down the street or just plain ignores me. I wouldn't want his job, it's a real dead end, if you know what I mean." They all shared a good laugh.

As they were chitchatting away, Lucy knocked on the door to announce the ME had arrived. Doctor Stefan Low was a character in action. He stood about five feet eight inches tall, about 150 pounds, with long uncombed curly graying hair. He recognized everyone and took a seat in the empty chair left at the round table.

After two hours of talk, back and forth, Fundalee announced the meeting was over. Jacob left the DA's office with a feeling of contentment. He knew his cooperation had gained grounds with the authorities. To him, as an investigator, this meant better and quicker access to information not available to the average person. He had strengthened his position and was happy about it.

As he got out of his car from the parking lot at the rear of his building, he saw a reflection in the window of a car a few spaces away that made his military instinct jump to the forefront. He ducked, hit the pavement, and at the same time pulled out his .45 as bullets hit his car. A fast moving car sped away with tires squealing. Jacob was able to catch the three digits of the license plate but not the letters. It was a California plate and he made a mental note of it. As he got up, he realized he must be more alert in the future. Fortunately, no one was around who could have been hit by a stray bullet. The PI ran to the rear door of the office building just as people were coming out to investigate what the shooting was all about. He was up the stairs in a jiffy and through the office door so fast, Anne barely had time to say hello.

The secretary said, "What made you rush so much, someone running after you or something?" she asked.

Jacob answered, "Somebody was taking pot shots at me on the parking lot. Get me Lieutenant Jones on the telephone, please."

"Are you hurt or just mad?" Anne questioned. She knew something had excited him, good or bad, and it appeared to have made him angry.

"Well, Lieutenant," Jacob said, "I don't think we have the right person behind bars for the murder of Louis 'The snake.' Unless somebody out there really hates me. Just a few minutes ago, after my return from the meeting with the DA and the ME, as I was getting out of my car in the parking lot at the back of my building, someone took four shots at me. I saw the make of the car and got the three digits from the license plate as I lay on the pavement, but did not see a face. You think you could match these numbers to a black 1946 Plymouth?" Jacob asked.

The lieutenant said, "You didn't even take a breath to give me a chance to talk. Do you think this was aimed at eliminating you or just scaring you? If it's the latter, whoever it was doesn't know you very well. Let me check on these numbers and I'll get back to you pronto."

Jacob was doing some deep thinking when Anne knocked on the door and came in with telephone messages. She was also curious as to what happened to her boss. Anne questioned, "What happened to you downstairs to make you so angry? Was someone shooting at you?"

"I think someone is trying to make a point, Anne. I wish I knew what it is they want and who that someone is. I thought with the arrest of Tony Padilla all attempts directed toward me would stop. Boy, did I guess wrong," Jacob said. "I hope you are being careful when you leave this place, Anne. Not that I think you're in danger, but one never knows what these low life people will do. Trying to scare me won't work, so they may think of using you as a means to get to me. Please be careful and be aware of your surroundings. Maybe you should take a week off until the lieutenant and I can sort this out."

As he finished his sentence, the telephone rang. Anne picked it up from his desk. "Jacob Schreiber private investigator, oh yes, Lieutenant, he's right here."

"That was fast, Bill, did you get a make on the plate? You say there's a possibility of two. Let's have them both. Oh! I see. One is in Northern California and the other one… Bingo," Jacob exclaimed. "That's our man, or I should say my man. It was not too smart of Paluka to have the goon use his own car. You're going to check it out and let me know. Thanks for your help, old friend." Jacob put the receiver back in its cradle. Anne was still standing there with her eyebrows raised.

"Don't you think you should tell me who this Paluka is, Jacob?"

"He's the guy who owns a pawnshop about four blocks away from here. Jack Paluka is a known associate of Tony Padilla. Bookies in the Hollywood area turned their cash over to him, otherwise they could not operate. As I suggested, Anne, why don't you take a week off, with pay of course, and call me by this time next week? We should have it all under wrap."

CHAPTER FIFTEEN...

The half-hour walk from his apartment to his office on Hollywood Boulevard gave Jacob the necessary time to plan his day. The shooting on the parking lot caused him to be more alert. Lieutenant Jones had confirmed Jack Paluka owned the car, but there was a snag in the whole thing. The day before the shooting, Paluka had reported the car stolen. Now both the lieutenant and Jacob knew this was a Mafia strategy. The plan had been set to hit the victim and in case of a foul up, a false report to the police would help the culprit establish his alibi. They were thinking all right, but not intelligently enough to fool Lieutenant Jones and Jacob.

He was a block away from his office when he saw what looked like Paluka's car driving slowly near the curb. Jacob eased himself in the entrance of a 24-hour coffee shop. From inside he was able to watch the car drive by with two goons in the front. It was the right car, and he was sure they were looking for him. He picked up the pay phone next to him and dialed the Lieutenant's private line.

"The car is going west on Hollywood, just saw him coming and ducked in to call you. Looks like they're going to make a right on Cahuenga. Yes, Bill, it's the same license number. What's that, you say someone broke in my office again? I better hurry and get there." Jacob walked out of the coffee shop with a paper cup in hand. He kept looking behind him to make sure he was not being followed. When he arrived at his office building, he noticed a commotion at the front door.

"What's going on, Officer? Did someone get hurt or what?" Jacob asked the police officer standing at the door checking people trying to walk in.

"Good morning, Mr. Schreiber, you're not going to like what you'll see when you get upstairs. Somebody broke into your office and trashed it. There are a couple of officers up there, I'm sure the sergeant knows you," the officer concluded as he moved aside to let Jacob walk in.

When he got up there, he could not believe the mess. Someone had used an axe and probably a sledgehammer to destroy his office furniture. The filing cabinet had been opened and spilled over. Files were all over the place. They had tried but didn't succeed in opening the safe. Most likely ran out when someone asked what was going on and called the police. Jacob was mad because he knew what they were looking for. The books with names and addresses of contacts for military weapons he had stashed in his safe. He went to the safe, opened it and was glad to see everything was there, including the envelopes containing the 75 grand he had taken away from Louis' safety deposit box.

The police sergeant said, "Somebody wanted to redecorate your office, Jacob. Whoever it was needs to take lessons in home and office décor. Do you happen to have unhappy clients, or do you think this is revenge?" asked the officer.

Jacob answered, "Sergeant, someone is not happy with me. This only makes it worse for them since I believe I know who did it. As long as no one is hurt, furniture can always be replaced. My insurance is up to date. Thanks for coming up here. Anything I can answer for you to complete your report?" Jacob concluded.

"Yes," said the police sergeant. "you can tell me who you think did this and my men and I can go give him a talking to or arrest him, if you are willing to press charges."

"I believe you know Jack Paluka, the man who owns a pawn shop not far from here. Why don't you go and harass him a bit? I don't have the proof yet it's actually him who did this, but I know it is. What he was looking for is in my safe, which they could not open since I have a triple combination on it, and it is welded onto the steel girders inside the wall. You could ask him what his car was doing driving away from this building a short time ago. He had reported the vehicle stolen a few days ago. You could ask him if the police had returned it to him. I'd be interested to know how he got it back so quick."

THE BOOKIE

Once the police officers left, Jacob called a friend in the office furniture business to replace what had been trashed. Putting the files back in proper order would be more tedious, so he placed everything together back into the filing cabinet. Anne would take care of it when she returned. The lieutenant had told him earlier they didn't have sufficient evidence to arrest and charge Paluka in the murder of Louis Billings. The same went for his participation in the military weapons theft. It was a question of time before they could pin something down on this slime ball. Eventually they all make mistakes, Bill Jones had said. Paluka was just a bit more careful than the others were, but he was getting closer to making a big mistake.

When Jacob arrived at Lorraine's place for dinner, he was carrying a dozen roses and two bottles of California wine. He had decided to give the boy an old glove he had for years. In fact, he told Gerald, "This is the glove I played Little League with; my father gave it to me. It's well-oiled and since I don't use it any more, you can have it for yourself, if you want."

"Gee, thanks, coach, this will be great," said a sparkling faced boy. He ran to his room and came back with a baseball to throw in the glove as all kids do to imitate big league players.

His mother said, "Remember, son, this is to play with outside at the ball park. Just be careful you don't throw it around in the house and break something." Lorraine turned to Jacob and gave him a big smile. "Thanks, Mr. Schreiber," she said coyly.

Jacob said, "You're both welcome. It was nothing really, a few flowers and an old glove I just kept for sentimental reasons. Gerald will get good use out of it. May I boldly ask what's for dinner? My concern is about the wine; did I bring the right kind? No need to be worried about my eating habits. I'll eat just about anything. From the wonderful odors I caught when I walked in, I gather you use herbs. No criticism, just wanted to let you know I have a passion for different herbs, that's all."

Lorraine was in a playful mood and enjoyed teasing Jacob. "Let me check with the chef and see what's on the menu for tonight. If we were all Catholics, this being Friday, fish would be the main dish, but since I'm not a religious person, I thought seafood would be appropriate."

They both burst out laughing. It was obvious they enjoyed each other's company. Jacob offered to open one of the wine bottles.

"Let's sit in the living room while the rice is cooking," Lorraine said. "I heard on the radio there was another incident in your office building. The reporter said that one of the offices on the second floor was trashed and the furniture smashed beyond recognition. I hope it wasn't your office, Jacob!"

"Unfortunately for me, it was. Someone thinks that I scare easy and wanted to make a point. The good side of all this is, I happen to know who had it done. My friend the lieutenant has probably paid him a visit by now. Bill Jones has a way of doing things that people will not forget. He hates cowards. People who do this sort of thing are cowards, hypocrites who hide in the dark or hang around in pairs to scare or beat other people up. My new furniture will all be in by Monday. I decided, since I had to replace most everything, to go modern this time around. I don't think any of these goons will be knocking on my office door anytime soon."

Gerald came rushing into the living room with his glove and ball in hand. "Mom, can I call my friend Teddy? You know, he's on the team with me. Me and him could go throw a few balls after dinner."

Lorraine took a quick glance at Jacob, who nodded his head.

"Sure, son, you can call your friend, but I don't want you to play in the street. Just go to the park across the street, it's safer there to play ball." Gerald rushed to the telephone. "This Teddy was here a couple of times and seems to be a nice boy. I'm sure happy we decided to go to the practice the other day. For Gerald to join your team has been a morale booster for him. Finding out his dad was not coming back from the war has been very hard on him. I'm very thankful for the day I walked in your office with my problem. You have a way of fixing things, Mr. Schreiber," she concluded with a grin on her face.

"What's this 'Mr. Schreiber' bit? Please call me Jacob. Otherwise I'll have to go back home and put my tux on to really make it formal." They both laughed again and seemed to be enjoying teasing one another. Lorraine noticed Jacob was not wearing his heavy artillery tonight. She didn't mind, as this made her realize the man was human after all and not a robot.

Dinner was been pleasant with lots of conversation from everyone and shared laughing. Once Gerald left to go play outside, Lorraine suggested they sit on the balcony. That way she could keep an eye on her young son across the street. She turned some soft music on and they took their wine to the balcony. Without saying anything, Jacob was enjoying being with Lorraine. He had not kissed her yet. He knew the proper time would come and did not want to rush things. It would not be right for him at this time, so he felt. The evening passed on too quickly and before they both realized, the late news was on television.

Jacob said, "I really want to thank you for a fabulous dinner and a wonderful evening. If you agree, the next one will be on me. The three of us could go to Chasen's in Beverly Hills. How about next Saturday? That should give you enough time to change your mind."

"Next Saturday will be wonderful," Lorraine said.

When Jacob arrived near his apartment building, he did his usual scouting to see if strange cars were parked close by. This time the coast was clear, so he proceeded to his regular parking space. Again, as he got out of the car and walked toward the entrance, he was careful to look around him. He certainly did not want surprises of the kind he got at the office parking lot a few days ago. He walked in, then closed and locked the door behind him. His apartment was on the third floor, which happened to be the top floor. He noticed the small piece of metal he always placed at the top of his door was still in place. This reassured him that no one had tried to force the door open or jimmy the lock to come in. He had just turned the lights on when the telephone rang. He looked at his watch, 12:35 AM. Jacob wondered who could be calling at this late hour.

"Schreiber here," he answered. "Oh! It's you, Lieutenant. Don't you ever take time to relax, have a beer, take your wife to a movie or just go to dinner?" he asked with a smile in his voice.

Lieutenant Jones said, "There was a big fire at a well-known pawnshop tonight. The Fire Chief says it smelled of arson all the way. Strong odors of kerosene and gasoline too. I believe the inner war has started amongst former friends and partners. Now that they all know Tony Padilla is not coming back soon, some of these hot heads want to establish a new executive, so to speak. Jack Paluka was not well liked amongst the regular thieves. He was feared because of his close association with Padilla. Big Tony being put away, this changes all the rules now. Whoever shows the strongest arm will become top dog. Paluka never had finesse or any diplomacy. Compromising was at the bottom of his priority list. Since he doesn't have Tony and his boys to defend him, he was the first to be hit. There was another hit after the fire began, this time on Wilshire Boulevard in a well-known gang hangout. Two thugs will be pushing daisies and fear struck the rest of the patrons. I wanted you to be aware of the gang activities. On a request from the FBI, we arrested Jack Paluka tonight. This all happened before his place was torched. Lucky for him or he would have been roasted too."

Jacob said, "You know, Lieutenant, it's always nice to hear the good news from a reliable source." They both laughed and said good night.

CHAPTER SIXTEEN...

When Anne returned to the office, it was Wednesday morning just before 8 o'clock. She was taken aback and for a split second thought she had entered a different office. The furniture was all new and modern. New padded chairs were there to make it more comfortable for clients. Jacob was right behind her and his usual good morning confirmed she was in the right place. "What happened here, I go away for a few days and come back to a refurbished office. What made you decide to change everything, Jacob?"

"You obviously did not listen to the news recently. While we were both away from the office, thank God, someone decided to redecorate the place. I arrived here the morning after you left and found the premises occupied by two LAPD officers who had been called by the building janitor when he heard a series of unusual crashing noises. Someone used an axe and a sledgehammer to destroy the furniture. When you open your new filing cabinet, you'll notice the files are just loose and 'confused' in there. Everything was all over the floor; I just picked it up carefully and placed it in the drawer. You'll have a week of filing to bring order to this mess. How do you like your new desk and highback chair? Pretty fancy, isn't it. A new modern telephone with two lines should do the trick for us, don't you think, Anne?"

Anne said, "You sure went all out, and you know what, I like it. Looks great. Did they catch the perpetrators?"

"I believe they did, Anne. Lieutenant Jones called me late the other night to inform me Jack Paluka had been booked on a charge of conspiracy to commit a federal offense for his part in the theft of military weapons from southern California establishments. His boys were seen leaving this building. They were in such a hurry, they left the axe and sledgehammer behind. Prints lifted from the handles matched a couple of goons who were in Mr. Paluka's employ. The pawnshop a few blocks away was torched last weekend. Before the firefighters could get there, it burned to the ground. Someone in the new upcoming underworld does not like Paluka. They probably thought they were rid of him at the same time. What no one knew was that Paluka had been arrested just hours before the place was torched. Lucky for him, or maybe not. His future, one way or the other, does not look too rosy." Jacob paused for a moment, admiring his new decorated office. *Nice*, he thought, *very nice*.

Anne was just taking her first sit down when the telephone rang. She pressed the flashing light and answered, "Schreiber investigations. He is in, could you hold the line please? Jacob, this is a Mr. Bill Watts. For some reason the name sounds familiar."

"Good morning, Mr. Watts. What brings you to my world of misfits?" Jacob listened for a while to what Bill Watts, the internationally renowned designer, was telling him. "Oh, I see. Well, I could come by this morning, say around ten-thirty. Good, I'll see you then."

Bill Watts owned a two-story former warehouse in Hollywood, where he had his atelier and produced his designs for both women's and men's clothing. Recently there had been a break-in, and some specific designs of men trousers had been stolen. Mr. Watts was not too worried about that because he could recreate the designs. What was bothering him is that he found out his stolen designs were showing up as finished products under a different label in stores across the Midwest and Eastern seaboard. He wanted Jacob to investigate the matter at any cost, he had said. Therefore, they would meet again at his residence in Beverly Hills in two hours.

He informed Anne who Bill Watts was and told her about the conversation. "I think you could open a new file on Mr. Designer," he said to Anne. "I have the feeling this is going to be a long, if not very long, working relationship. In the meantime, I hope we can close the file on Louis 'The Snake' Billings. Thirty-five hundred dollars of new furniture, not including the repairs to the office itself, adds up quick. I took it out of the slush fund in the safe. Do you think it would be safer to transfer the money from the safe to a separate bank account?"

Anne replied, "It would at least earn interest instead of being stagnant. Yes, I think you should place it in your account. No need for a different account. You can classify it as money in transit from a client or just as fees received."

Jacob agreed with Anne's comments. "When I come back from my meeting with Mr. Watts, we can go to the bank together."

When Jacob arrived at the Watts address in Beverly Hills, it was the same scenario as the previous time. Ring the intercom, announce who you are and the gate opens. This time he drove all the way to the front of the mansion and parked at the curb of the circular driveway. The butler, a medium-sized Negro, perfectly suited in dress pants and matching vest with white hair and a limp in his walk, was there to receive him. He escorted Jacob to a closed door on which he knocked and announced that Mr. Jacob Schreiber had arrived.

"Come in, Mr. Schreiber, make yourself comfortable. James, would you bring us a fresh pot of coffee and a cup for Mr. Schreiber? I am not usually here at this time of the morning, but my assistant is taking care of business in Hollywood." Bill Watts thought for a moment then said, "It could be quite devastating for me and the people with whom I do business if the copies of my designs are put out on the market illegally."

Jacob asked, "When did you first notice your designs were missing?"

"About six to seven weeks ago when I returned from my European trip with Earl. Three days after you were here, a close friend brought over a pair of trousers he had purchased in Boston. They didn't have my label but looked similar to my own production. I called the store owner in Boston and we had a nice conversation. He also buys my products for one of his clothing brands. He said he would check with his purchasing manager and get back to me as soon as he could. Well, it was three days later and by that time several more copies arrived at my shop. The Boston store-purchasing manager gave me the information where he purchased for the store and the name of the contact person. The trousers looked just like my designs, except for the inside stitching. It does not have the same pattern or quality as mine do. I'm telling you, Mr. Schreiber, this is highway robbery. I called the number of the supplier and when I tried to find information on its ownership and physical address, I was rudely cut off. I have set money aside for a thorough investigation should you decide to take me on as a client. This envelope has a check made out to you for $15,000, a retainer to begin investigating. What do you say to my offer, Mr. Schreiber?"

"I will need a list of all your employees, basically a personnel file on each and every one would be helpful. I will also want the contact person and telephone number of the Boston store as well as the information he gave you. Once I have gone through the personnel files, I would want a personal tour of your working facility. How soon can you get those files to me?" Jacob asked.

Watts said, "I will have the files of my eleven employees in your office by 3 o'clock today." The designer passed a sheet of paper and the check to Jacob across his desk. "Whatever cooperation you will need, I'll do my best to make sure you get, and fast. Whoever did this has to be brought to justice and the sweatshop operators have to be put in jail. They operate illegally, probably don't pay taxes and most likely employ unregistered migrants for wages next to nothing. There is the smell of some organized crime behind it all. I certainly hope you find the culprits. As I said earlier, I couldn't afford to have this kind of theft affect my business. I'm sorry if I rattle on, Mr. Schreiber, but I'm very upset over this incident. Thank you for responding positively," concluded the designer.

"I'll keep you up to date on the progress of my investigation as the need arises. Anything urgent you will hear from me immediately. Thank you for your trust, I certainly will do my best to live up to it," Jacob said as he got up to leave.

On his return trip to the office, the PI thought about his meeting with Bill Watts. He probably would have to go east unless he could locate a trusted colleague and subcontract some work to him.

Anne was waiting for him when he walked in. "How did your meeting go?" she asked. "Did you get a new client signed on? It

THE BOOKIE

sounds interesting to deal with a designer, don't you think so, Jacob?"

Jacob just waved the fifteen thousand-dollar check at her. "Here is the beginning of a fruitful association. I'm glad I left my business card at Bill Watts' place when I located Earl Edwards," he said as he handed Anne the check. "We could go to the bank now and I'll fill you in on the information you will need to know for this case, my dear secretary." They both left with a bag full of money and a major check to deposit at the same time.

"Did you know that Hollywood Park, aside from horse races, has a wonderful restaurant? Could I talk you into having lunch there with me today, and no, they don't serve horse meat," Jacob said with a smile.

"You're on, Mr. Investigator. Best offer I had in a long time," Anne said laughing out loud.

They both hurried to the bank less than one block from the office, carrying 75 Gs in a paper bag and a check for 15 Gs. When they sat with the regular bank vice-president, it took but ten minutes to complete the transaction. Jacob had been dealing at the same bank since before joining the Marines in '41.

"Let's walk to my car and I'll drive you to where those who dream of horses spend their daylight hours hoping the one they chose will come in first. It can be a happy place, if you win, and a very depressing one if you don't. For some people the latter is what happens most of the time," Jacob explained.

During lunch Jacob briefed Anne on the Watts' file and Joan Libbit's upcoming divorce case. He told his secretary to hire a photographer they had used before who knew the ropes in the investigating business. "Sometimes" he said, "you have to stretch the truth in order to get what you need." He wanted Anne to coordinate the Libbit case. She was good at this and knew how to approach people to get the most out of them. Libbit's Trucking Company had a fifteen-acre lot and warehouse in Newhall, just north of the San Fernando Valley. They also had another depot in Orange County to make it easier to access the southern routes going east. Both facilities would have to be visited. According to Joan Libbit, her husband had a yacht anchored in Long Beach, where he did most of his partying.

Two hours later they returned to the office, satisfied with a good working lunch. Jacob had a habit of doing this. He liked to use his time fully, lunch without a good conversation was like having a meal without seasoning, he always commented.

Once in the office, Jacob called Anne for more conversation. "My dear secretary" he said, "with some of the money we deposited today I'm going to establish a slush fund. By that, I mean an available source of cash to cover the cost of investigating cases for people who cannot legitimately afford to pay. Case in point, Lorraine Buford. When you feel, and I trust your judgement on this, that a client is in desperate need of my services but cannot pay my going rate, we will use the resources of the fund. Does it sound clear to you, or would you put it some other way?" Jacob said.

Anne said, "Many times in the past I'm sure there were prospective clients we could have helped but didn't. Now that you bring this up, I can see where, in specific cases, we can do much good. You are one heck of a boss, Jacob Schreiber."

CHAPTER SEVENTEEN...

The Little League practice last Wednesday night had gone well. The whole club was upbeat. Everyone had concentrated on the instructions of the coach and followed his command to the letter. If only they would do the same under real game conditions, but children are what they are. There are times their attention span is not very lengthy. Today was Saturday, opening day for the kids. It was exciting to wear your new uniform the first time around. The uniform consisted of a jersey and hat. It was the first real game of the season for everyone. There were ceremonies like in the big ballparks. The president addressed the parents and barely touched on the kids. The Campagnos (Lilly and Joseph) sang the national anthem. William Chaffers, a movie star in demand, pitched the first ceremonial ball to the mayor of Los Angeles. Both individuals had a kid of their own in the league. As usual, the sun was shining high in the sky, and the day announced itself as a wonderful one. Even the hot dog vendor was in a happy mood on this special day. Hot dogs with all the trimmings were a nickel apiece. In short, it was the best day of the summer season so far.

Jacob's team was the best of the lot. Gerald turned out to be an excellent shortstop and a prolific hitter. He had two home runs and two triples to help his team win 9-2. As he had done at the practice, Jacob invited the whole team to hot dogs and since they were only a nickel each, the big spender didn't have to put out a lot of money. The first official day of Little League baseball was a success in many ways.

When Jacob arrived at the office on Monday morning, Anne was there writing down messages she wanted her boss to handle. Two calls from back east in reference to his new client, the designer. The first one was from a private eye in Boston by the name of Jake.

"This is Jacob Schreiber in Los Angeles, Jake. I was wondering if you could do some legwork for me. Since it's out of my territory, I would like to hire you for that part of the work. Would you prefer a flat fee or an hourly rate?" Jacob asked. "Oh, I see. Well, it won't be that difficult for you since you live there and know the parties involved." Jacob gave the contact person and a general overview of what the case was about and what he was looking for.

Jake said, "How about a three hundred dollar flat fee including expenses? If I run into a more extensive search, I'll let you know."

Jacob's second call was to New York City, to the head of the association of the garment district. That call proved a bit more difficult and Jacob concluded he would have to fly to New York and meet this person face-to-face. He had gone through the eleven files delivered to him from Bill Watts' place of business.

Now he wanted Anne to go through every one of the personnel files. She made notes on length of employment, previous employment, home addresses and telephone numbers. Anything she found that did not appear to fit within the context of that person's background, she red-flagged. Out of the eleven, three had been arrested for a variety of offences, including drunk driving. The three names were marked on a separate list with their SSN to be verified with the sheriff's department, the bureau of prisons and the Attorney General's office. So far, nothing dramatically suspicious had shown up. A visit to the working warehouse by Jacob might change that. A case with this kind of industrial espionage was never easy to prove. It usually was an inside job. In the majority of cases, where there were thefts of money, whether embezzled or physically taken, it was greed by a trusted employee. The garment industry did not have a reputation of crooked management, but it did have a bad reputation when it came to the quality of employees it hired. Low wages and foreign workers were always fertile grounds for illegal activities. The Mafia had begun looking into the garment business. It is big business. When you think of all the stores nationwide being supplied by small manufacturers, the cash flow was in the tens of millions on an annual basis. In New York especially, where the different 'families' controlled given areas, the garment district was

THE BOOKIE

considered very big business.

Jacob decided to call his friend the lieutenant. "How's your day going so far, Bill? Anyone ever told you not to work so hard? Could I ask you to verify some names for me, three would be max for now. I'll ask Anne to give you the details, and yes, I'll owe you one, friend!"

The lieutenant answered, "Glad to oblige, my friend. By the way, Paul Trickten turned some interesting papers over to me. It's a list of names with telephone numbers of people who dealt in stolen goods for our friend Paluka. There is a name on that list you might be interested to look at. You once asked me about Earl Edwards. What in the world is the son of an oil millionaire from Texas doing with the likes of Paluka? His name was amongst others with a telephone number in Dallas. Was he buying drugs from him or stolen property of some kind? It may be nothing at all, Jacob, but one never knows. This kid is a high roller, so my feeling is that he was looking for drugs. By the way, before I forget to tell you, the Feds have dropped the murder charge on Padilla. They are going to stick to the narcotics and weapons dealing. I think that it's their best chance of getting a conviction, don't you?" asked an upbeat lieutenant.

"I agree," Jacob said. "About Earl Edwards, I find it interesting his name should pop up in the most unusual place. I'm going to have a serious look into this, Lieutenant. We know the old saying, 'where there's smoke, there's fire.' Now that I think of it, I wonder how his father happened to come right up to my office the day he was looking for him. It almost sounds like a conspiracy to involve me without my having full knowledge of the purpose behind the whole thing. What do you think, Lieutenant?" the gumshoe concluded.

"There could be something not too kosher," said the detective. "If I were you, Jacob, I would be very careful in my dealings with any of the oil rich Edwards.' Sometimes the motive behind an incident does not surface until much later in the investigation. How about we meet for coffee and doughnuts at the Santa Monica Pier tomorrow, the treat's on me this time," Jones said.

"Best offer I've had this week, Lieutenant. I'll see you bright and early tomorrow at the usual place."

After he hung up, Jacob began to think about Earl Edwards and his association with Jack Paluka. Was it drugs? Was it gambling? Was it stolen goods? Then a thought crossed Jacob's mind about Bill Watts. Whoever stole his designs had to be someone who had access to his work. Maybe someone close who did not cause alarm for anyone to suspect bad intentions. *First things first*, he said to himself. A visit to Watts' place of business was really the first step in this investigation. He picked up the telephone again and dialed Bill Watts' number.

"Jacob Schreiber here, may I speak with Mr. Watts please?" He waited what seemed an awful long time before the designer answered. "Would this afternoon be a good time to come visit your work shop?" the private eye asked.

Watts answered, "I'll make sure I'm here for you, Mr. Schreiber. What time is convenient for you? Good, I'll see you around three then."

"Anne, I need the personnel files on the Watts case," Jacob called out. "Before you give it back to me, could you call Lieutenant Jones and give him those three names and Social Security Numbers? Sorry, I hung up too eagerly. I'm going to the designer's work place here in Hollywood this afternoon. Anything you would like me to order for you?" he added with a smile on his face.

Anne answered, "Yes, Jacob, why don't you bring me back a long black evening dress, size three. Tell him to send you the bill," she quipped. Humor had always been part of their work place. She didn't mind at all. In fact, she enjoyed it a lot. It kept a balance in the seriousness of the daily routine. Not that she found her work boring, on the contrary, she found it too active at times.

Jacob was given a grand tour of Watts Enterprises as it was called. He briefly met each of the eleven employees Every person knew why he was visiting Watts Enterprises. Bill Watts had informed everyone in a general meeting that some of his designs had been stolen from the premises. Jacob Schreiber had been hired to investigate the matter. The designer told his employees he had preferred a private investigator with the reputation of Mr. Schreiber instead of having a police investigation for now. Therefore, no one was surprised when they were called in to a private talk with the investigator.

It took Jacob about three hours to talk with everyone. He made notes of the information given to him by the workers. Nothing out of the ordinary surfaced during the questioning and this made him wonder if Watts had been hiding some facts from him. He would get back to that touchy point later. He thanked the designer for his cooperation in organizing the participation of the employees and told him he would find his way out.

As he got to the door, it was locked and he could not open it. A voice behind him said, "Hold on a moment, sir, I'll let you out." Jacob turned around and saw a tall Negro wearing a hat on which the insignia said, 'Golden Security.'

"I suppose you work here on a part-time basis," Jacob said.

"Oh! No, sir, I work here every night, six nights a week. My name is Paul and may I ask who you are?"

"You certainly may, Paul, I'm Jacob Schreiber, private investigator. Mr. Watts hired my services to find out who stole some of his designs. Are you aware there had been a theft in here some weeks back?"

"Yes, sir, I have been told that, but as I said to my supervisor, the only people I've seen here at night are either Mr. Watts or his friend Mr. Earl. You see, Mr. Earl, when he's in town, comes in and out of here with Mr. Watts and sometimes returns alone later the same night."

Jacob asked, "Did you ever see him carrying a large briefcase or one of those large portfolio carriers I saw in the office upstairs when Mr. Earl left the building?"

Paul answered, "Mr. Earl always carried something with him, whether he was with Mr. Watts or not. You see, Mr. Schreiber, my shift is from four to midnight. Many times Mr. Earl was here by himself when I left. He had the keys to lock the place."

"Thanks, Paul, you have been very helpful to me. If I have any more questions I know when and where to get you," Jacob said as he left the building.

Funny, he thought, *that Bill Watts never mentioned Earl Edwards doing some work for him, I wonder why.* He wondered if a trip to New York was necessary. What he needed the most right now was a photograph of Earl Edwards. Then he remembered his father had left two 8x10's with him. On his way to the office he tried to push away the fact Earl could be the guilty party in this investigation. Jacob would have to find out more before coming to any conclusion. Especially since Watts and Edwards were lovers, it brought some sensitivity to his approach. He would send one of the pictures to his contact in Boston by overnight courier. There may be nothing to this angle but one never knows. *Greed, anger and jealousy will make a person do things that they would not normally do,* Jacob thought. Watts must have known about Earl going to the workshop after hours. Maybe he did some of the design work for him. Jacob recalled the older Edwards telling him how talented his son was in the arts. "Maybe," he said aloud, "I'm making too much out of this."

CHAPTER EIGHTEEN...

Jacob had never complained to the authorities about the way they handled murder investigations. The Louis Billings investigation, though, was bothering him. After all, the body had been left on his office floor. That alone made it too personal. These thoughts were going through his head as he was staring at the ocean, waiting for his friend the lieutenant to show up. Coffee and doughnuts on him, he had said.

Jacob was not a procrastinator. When he had a new client, the first thing he liked to do was check the facts given to him by the client. Then, he put the wheels in motion, looking for new evidence or anything related to the case in question to build his file. Because of his attention to small details, many customers came back to him for either a similar or a different type of investigation. He was now able to sustain himself, a well-paid secretary, and make a profit. He would soon be able to buy a house and pay cash for it. The private eye already had in mind the area where he wanted to live. Northwest of the San Fernando Valley, a new area called Northridge had appealed to him.

Leaning over the railing, watching the white caps on the ocean allowed him to let his mind wander.

"A penny for your thoughts, mister gumshoe," said the lieutenant as he spotted Jacob. "You didn't think I would make it, did you now?" said a cheerful detective. "Maybe we ought to sit on the bench at the end of the pier, out of earshot, so we can have a quiet, undisturbed conversation. my friend."

Jacob answered, "It sounds good to me, Lieutenant. A slight breeze will not bother us. I have the feeling you want to tell me something!"

"I do. Jacob, whether it's important to you or not depends on how you feel about the LAPD. Let's get the conversation tools," he said as he directed the walk towards the coffee and doughnuts stand. They walked to the end of the pier in silence. Bill Jones had been in the police force eleven years now. His only outside-the-force friendship was Jacob, whom, at times, he trusted more than some of his own men. The Santa Monica Pier was always an ideal place for private talk. Not too many people around and a few places to sit down.

Unexpectedly Jacob started the conversation. "The information you gave me about Earl Edwards and his name being amongst many others in one of Paluka's little black books is turning out to be significant. I see you raising your eyebrows, wondering why I would bring this up. Well, Lieutenant, I have a new client who has a problem with at least one of his designs being stolen from his workshop. There could be more, but he won't know that for some time yet. Have you heard of Bill Watts of Beverly Hills? He's a women's and men's clothing designer. His preference in lovers is men. Young men like Earl Edwards. Now your face shows interest and inquisitiveness at the same time. I was just wondering if our friend Earl is a gambler or drug addict. It's rather difficult to know that unless we have some proof or information as to his kinky habits. Maybe from the Dallas Police department? Is there someone you could contact and find out if someone just happens to have a rap sheet on Edwards? What do you think, Lieutenant?"

Bill Jones had listened well, but now was eager to talk. "My intentions today were somewhat different than the subject you just brought up, Jacob. I know that not knowing why Louis 'The Snake' was dropped in your office has been bothering you since the day it happened. I'm still working on that. We strongly believe Padilla ordered the hit. We also know that Louis had been skimming off the top from the weapons deals, and that could be the reason why he was eliminated. What none of us knows is the obvious, why place the body in your office? Several scenarios come to mind when we think about who you are and what you do for a living. The possibility of you knowing about Padilla's little guerrilla warfare and how the stolen military arms got by customs is the number one of all scenarios possible. You finding all those books, the briefcase and other things, tends to actually authenticate the scenario, wouldn't you think?" Bill Jones said.

"Yes it does, Lieutenant," said the gumshoe. "But what you seem to forget is that I found all the information after the fact. There has to be another motivator than this one. Padilla is a smart man. Like all smart criminals he was caught. The only reason he was caught so quickly is the information I turned over to you and to the FBI. For me to find what I found was just a stroke of luck. Again, Bill, this all happened after Louis' dead body was dumped on me. You took a chance the day you arrested Black Jack Tony in his limousine in front of my office building. Lucky for you and me the FBI was ready to swing into action. Otherwise, Tony Padilla would have his freedom and would be causing us more problems. No, I don't think your scenario is the key as to why the body was left in my office," concluded the private investigator.

"What else could it be? Padilla, for whatever reason, was sure you had information that could jeopardize his operation. Neither you nor I were aware of the illegal arms dealing until Paul Trickten told us. Then what we found in the books and papers made us realize the seriousness of these thefts. I still think Louis must have said something to Black Jack Tony to make him do what he did. Trashing your office and not finding what he was after most likely made him decide to throw a little fear in you. That is exactly what he wanted to do. He could have killed you quickly, but that would not have given him the papers he was after. Dumping Louis' body in your office was his way of telling you he knew something was going on, all the while hoping you would scare easy. I guess this is the best way I can explain it, Jacob."

They both finished the coffee and doughnuts and just sat silent for a few minutes.

Jacob said, "I understand your point of view, Bill. Still, I feel there is another motive behind all of this. We both think Padilla ordered the hit, since he's the godfather for southern California. But think for a moment, what if someone else wanted Louis 'The Snake' dead? Did you ever think of that possibility?"

The lieutenant answered, "To be honest with you, I didn't. I guess it's always easier to look at the obvious. I really can't see anyone outside Tony Padilla's family circle doing a major hit on one of the bookies. That, in their circles, would be the equivalent to signing your own death warrant. Do you have any particular individual in mind, Jacob?"

"Not really, Lieutenant, it's just a hunch, a real strong gut feeling. I understand the power Tony Padilla has, or should I say had in organized crime here in southern California. My point is that leaving a dead person's body in my office does not go along with Padilla's way of doing things. If he really thought I had something he wanted, he would have cornered me or kidnaped me and tried to make me talk. As a last resort, he would have killed me. Don't you see what I'm getting at, Lieutenant?" Jacob said.

"Yes I do, Jacob, but who would want, aside from Padilla, to make a statement of this sort? His men were involved, we know that. What we don't know is which one killed Louis. They transported his body to your office for a reason. However baffling it is, they had a reason for doing so. Your office was ransacked and they found nothing. Yet, when we checked his house, we found it in good order. As good as a single male's house could be. The comparisons may seem a little odd to you, but to us it is an indicator they were looking for something which was not at Louis' place of residence. They could not have known he had left a briefcase at his estranged wife's home the same night. That was what they were looking for. Padilla knew it contained the list of contacts for the arms sales. Because Louis did not want any physical harm done to Helen Billings, he must have told them you had what they were after. Don't you think this makes sense, Jacob?"

"It all makes sense, Lieutenant, but I'm still not happy with the conclusion you want to bring to the case. You are trying to convince me now that Padilla, Paluka and some of their cronies are in jail, possibly for a very long time, I should lay off the bookie's death. Is this what you are trying to do, my friend?"

"Not exactly, Jacob, I can't tell you to stop your search for truth if that is what you believe. I know you well enough to understand you won't stop looking until you are satisfied. What I'm saying is that we, and I hate to admit it even to you, are at a dead end in this investigation. There are no new clues to be pursued. There are no new witnesses coming forward. Because of all these factors, I'm closing the case for the time being. If you come up with new evidence and a new direction, I'll gladly look into it. That I can promise you, Jacob. There are so many cases surfacing every day, it's becoming a difficult task trying to investigate them all quickly. I have asked the chief for more manpower, but we know how that goes with the upper level politicians and their budget woes. It will take months, and only if I'm lucky, before anyone is transferred or added to my section. My priorities don't seem to matter much when they get to the top echelon of the LAPD. Because I consider you a friend, I just had to tell you face to face what my intentions were. I hope you'll understand my dilemma, Jacob. This does not mean we should stop cooperating, on the contrary, we should always have an open communication line between us," the lieutenant concluded.

"I can understand your restrictions, Bill. I'm glad they don't apply to me. My budget is far less than yours, but so are my restrictions. I am going to pursue the gut feeling I have until it fizzles out. If I find something interesting, you will be the first person to know. I do appreciate your open mind, and trust me, I feel the same way toward you. Our friendship should not be jeopardized by any incident, whether it's on my side of the fence or on your side of it."

The two friends left the pier together, then drove in different directions. Jacob was glad the lieutenant openly admitted his frustrations at not being able to fully clear the air about Louis Billings' murder case.

The private eye always enjoyed driving back to the office, as it gave him time to think. In the investigating business, the major portion of time spent by a gumshoe was analyzing the different possibilities. Thinking with a clear head was very important. As he drove in to the parking lot Jacob thought about his next move in the Watts' case. Something was nagging at him. Something the night watchman had told him when he last talked with him. When he entered the office, Anne greeted him in her usual cheerful way.

"Here is an important call for you," she said as she handed him the phone slip. Anne was in her mid-thirties, five feet three, about 110 pounds and married to a professor. She had a Bachelor of Science degree from UCLA. Anne had taken the job with Jacob because it was close to home, sounded intriguing and the pay offer was more than all the other places she had interviewed with. Her husband had met Jacob a few times and when she told him about the job offer, he was all for it. Schreiber was a friend of the dean of law where Anne's husband worked and often came to visit and talked about his Little League team. Anyone involved with kids playing ball cannot be that bad to work for, he had said to her. Her decision had been easy and she never looked back.

Jacob's important message was from Lorraine and when he dialed the number, he couldn't help but smile at the way Anne was playing cupid with him.

"This is Jacob, sorry I wasn't here when you called, but here I am."

"Hi, Jacob, I know you are very busy these days. I just wanted you to know my sister is arriving for a visit tomorrow. She'll probably be here for two weeks. Therefore, I thought I could get her to stay with Gerald this coming weekend. You mentioned wanting to go to La Jolla soon, did you not?"

"I sure did, Lorraine. This sounds like a perfect weekend to go south and get to know each other better. We have a practice on Wednesday and a game on Friday this week instead of Saturday. Your sister's timing is perfect. By the way, what's her name?"

"Colette is her name. She's a cheerful soul, laughing at everything and nothing. I think she wants to move to California soon. We will all see you at the ballpark on Wednesday," Lorraine concluded before saying goodbye.

Jacob just sat there enjoying the moment. He had been thinking about an approach to have Lorraine to himself for a weekend and here, unexpectedly, it fell on his lap. This sister deserved two hot dogs after the practice on Wednesday night.

CHAPTER NINETEEN...

"Good morning to you, Jake, this is Jacob Schreiber in Los Angeles. I sent you a photograph of a young man by the name of Earl Edwards yesterday. When you check with the purchasing agent of the two stores in Boston, could you ask if they recognize the person in the picture? It's just a hunch I have. Did you get the three hundred-dollar money order? Good, let me know whenever you have anything. You can call me collect if it's more convenient for you, and thanks again.

"Anne, could you get Leon Edwards on the telephone for me? If he isn't there, ask if they have a number for his son Earl."

Jacob sat there thinking about who would buy a stolen design and manufacture the garment in large quantities. He suddenly remembered a restaurant owner in Chinatown who had hired him to find two of his relatives. They had vanished on their way from San Francisco to his residence in southeast Los Angeles. The restaurant owner had paid several thousand dollars to a criminal Chinese organization to bring his two cousins here to work for him. Because they were females, he feared the Chinese gangsters had sold them to a sweatshop operator somewhere in East LA. Some three weeks after Jim Lee hired him, he located the girls with the help of Lieutenant Jones, rescued them, and closed the sweatshop down. The operator of the illegal shop was arrested, charged and paid a heavy fine. By now he probably was operating another sweatshop as most of these people do, since they're funded by organized crime. Jacob decided to visit Chinatown and have a talk with Jim Lee. He may have an answer to his question regarding sweatshops.

Anne came back to his office and said, "Leon Edwards is not available, but I have a number where to reach Earl, if you wish to do so, now or later, Mr. Gumshoe."

When he got to Jim Lee's restaurant, he found a parking space right at the front door, walked in and took a seat in the last booth near the kitchen door. When the waitress came to his booth, he handed her his card and ask for Jim Lee. The young woman looked at the card and with a worried look on her face hurried behind the doors to the kitchen.

"Mr. Schreiber, nice to see you today. May I offer you lunch with me," Jim Lee said with a big grin on his face.

Jacob answered, "It is very nice of you to offer me your hospitality, Jim Lee. Yes, I'll have a large bowl of wonton soup." He knew refusing Lee's hospitality would have been considered rude, if not an insult, to the establishment. "What I came to see you about is very important to me, Jim Lee. I believe you know how the sewing sweatshops operate, don't you?" the private eye asked.

Jim Lee said, "I know a little bit about them. You see, Mr. Schreiber, the Mexicans run these shops. They have girls from all over Mexico, and Chinese girls, too. All of them are here illegally and get little wages. The girls all live in houses provided by the shop operators, to whom they have to pay rent. Many of them end up on the street as prostitutes under a black pimp. You saved my two cousins from that terrible life, Mr. Jacob. I will tell you everything I know if it can help you." Jim Lee thought for a moment and then began his story. "The young girls become slaves, as they can never repay the high fees they are charged to come to America. They are told if they don't work in the shops to pay back their loan, they will either be turned over to the police, who in turn will have them deported back to China, or be killed. The fear these young women have prevents them from talking to anyone about their situation. This has been going on for a long time, Mr. Schreiber, and nobody in authority wants to put a stop to these sweatshops. The operators pay money to the local politicians to keep the police away from them. I heard stories that in order to really put fear in these girls, the owner beats one in front of the rest and tells them this would happen to them if they don't follow the rules. Many girls have disappeared under these circumstances, never to be found alive."

Jacob interrupted, "Jim Lee, what I would like to know is how and

THE BOOKIE

where do the operators get the work orders? Someone must bring them designs and patterns. Are these obtained by regular channels or by some other means? Do you know anything about that?"

Jim Lee looked around to make sure no one was close by. He leaned forward and spoke in a lower voice. "Mr. Schreiber, I don't know everything but I was once told that the patterns which they use are stolen from designers' work places. They are slightly modified and each pattern is reproduced by the thousand. From what I understand it's a multimillion dollar business." Still speaking in a low tone he added, "I was also told the Mafia has a hand in the rag business as they call it. It is a very dangerous thing to touch, Mr. Jacob. If I was you, I would stay away."

Jacob thanked him for the soup and left the restaurant. On his return to Hollywood he kept thinking about the sweatshop operation and how it could be interconnected with Paluka, Edwards and organized crime for that matter. He wondered if the dead bookie Louis 'The Snake' had a hand in that kind of operation too. The more he thought about it, the more confusing it became, unless... "Why did I not think of that before!" he exclaimed. "That has to be it. Earl Edwards, not the father, is the one involved with the Padilla family. I wonder if he already knows his friendly associates are all in jail. There's only one way to find out. Ask a direct question and you shall get an evasive answer."

As he pulled into the office parking lot, he noticed an ambulance with all its lights on in a flashing mode. There were two police cars as well as a LAFD truck with the tall ladder. *Something happened, hopefully not in my office this time around.* He rushed up the stairs, got to his door and there was Anne, calm as ever talking on the telephone.

She finished her conversation and before she could say anything, Jacob said, "What's going on with the ambulance and the police downstairs?" he asked.

Anne replied, "I was just about to tell you. The accountant on the third floor had a heart attack and a lawyer in the office next door to him broke his wrist trying to help the poor man. Nothing to do with us this time around, Mr. Schreiber. Aren't we lucky!" she said with a tone of humor in her voice.

Jacob sat at his desk, found the paper with Earl Edwards' telephone number on it and dialed. He got an answering service and left a message with his name and telephone number. A second visit to Watts' workshop would help him familiarize himself with the designing side of the clothing industry. When a thief takes something of value and resells it, the danger of that thief being found becomes much greater. There was a piece of the puzzle missing. Something was not right at Bill Watts' workshop. Jacob could not put his finger on it yet.

The telephone rang and Anne informed him young Edwards was on the line. "This is Jacob Schreiber. I was just curious as to when you are coming back to Los Angeles for a trip. No, nothing urgent, just wanted to have a talk with you. I'm interested in knowing more about the oil business and I figured it would be easier to talk to you about it than your father. So you say in about ten days. Good, give me a call when you get in town, if you have some time to chat about oil with me."

Jacob's quick thinking had provided him with a conversation piece without rousing any suspicion on Earl's side. Now he would have to ask Bill Watts not to let Earl know immediately about his investigating a possible case of industrial espionage in his shop. He didn't have concrete proof for the moment, but the comments from the security guard and his name being amongst a list of names carried by Jack Paluka cast a heavy shadow on his evening activities at the work plant.

Jacob arrived unannounced to see Bill Watts. He was made to wait for a short time. The secretary was aware of Jacob's business and curious if he had found a solution to the business problem. "Not yet, Miss," Jacob said. "Could you tell me if you have a telephone number in Dallas for Earl Edwards?"

"I do, let me right it down for you. Mr. Earl called yesterday when Mr. Watts was out of the building and ask to speak to Mario, you know, the floor foreman who basically runs the shop."

THE BOOKIE

Jacob said, "Did he say if he was coming to LA soon for a visit?"

The secretary answered, "Not to me, maybe if you ask Mario or Mr. Watts. He's free now, you may go in, Mr. Schreiber."

Bill Watts greeted Jacob with enthusiasm. "Anything of interest to report, Mr. Schreiber? I suppose you have some more questions to ask. As I said to you before, you don't need my permission to go in the workshop. Every employee has been told to cooperate with you."

"That part of it makes my life easier, thank you. What I need to ask you is rather sensitive because it touches you personally. I don't know any other way but straightforward when it comes to asking questions."

"Come now, Mr. Schreiber, I have nothing to hide, so you can ask me any question you want and I'll answer you just as straightforward."

Jacob was somewhat ill at ease, but he knew the questions would have to be asked eventually, so he braced himself and began. "Could you tell me what your relationship with Earl Edwards is, number one. Number two, does he do work on projects for you when he's here in LA? Number three, did you hear from him in the past week?"

"I guess you already know that my sexual preference is with men. Earl is just a young lover I picked up at the Brown Derby one day. As far as Earl doing any projects for me, I'll have to say no. Oh, he showed me some of his drawings at one time, but I told him his style did not come close to what I want to produce. Do you have something specific in mind? Is this why you're asking me about Earl? On your third question, the answer is no. I have been busy with preparing a fashion show for next month and have not had much time to socialize with anyone. It sounds to me as if there is something you are not telling me, Mr. Schreiber. Am I right to take this assumption?"

"Because of my contacts with the LAPD and other investigating agencies I have access to information some PI would find difficult to get on a moment's notice. I certainly don't want to alarm you, but rather caution you about Earl Edwards." Jacob went on to explain what he had found out from the night watchman regarding Earl being in the workshop after everyone had gone home for the day. He also explained to Watts the necessity for him to retain the same attitude so as not to alarm Earl in case his findings did not fully justify what he had just told him. "I have a couple of your employees I need to question again today. Whatever I find, I shall tell you before I leave the building. If you receive any unusual telephone calls or threats, I want you to find me right away. Here's a card with my home telephone number on it as well as my address. I have a feeling what is being stolen from you is also being done at other places. Have you heard from other designers with a similar problem?"

"Indeed I have," said the international designer. "I just didn't pay attention to it when two other top-notch designers told me, four to five months ago, they had been burglarized. Some of their modified designs were showing up nationwide. I did not think anything of it at the time. Now that you mention it, the whole situation comes back to me. What's amazing in all this, Mr. Schreiber, is that none of my original designs are missing. How could they have done it? It's a mystery to me and I hope you can find the guilty person or persons for that matter."

Jacob got up and left to go inside the workshop to talk to Mario and possibly Paul the security guard, if he was around. On his way to the workshop, he asked the secretary if, aside from the one call she had mentioned, Earl had called to talk to other employees. She told him yes, he had talked to Paul, the security guard twice or three times in the past two weeks.

The city gumshoe thanked her and asked that she keep this information confidential.

CHAPTER TWENTY...

After he left the designer's warehouse, Jacob went straight to his office. There was a lot of thinking to be done about this case. His talk with Mario, the shop foreman, had brought new information to the surface regarding Mr. Earl's activities. Furthermore, Paul the security guard had also told him about Edwards wanting to access the work place in the late evening. All this pointed to wrongful activities since the owner, Bill Watts, did not appear to be aware of his lover's plans. Paul had told Mr. Earl he would need to have written authorization from Mr. Watts to access the premises after working hours. In fact, Mario had shown Jacob a memo informing all employees there would be no access to the building after 5 PM. This recent memo was signed by Bill Watts and further said that any employee found on the premises or wanting to access the premises after closing time without written permission would be dismissed immediately.

Jacob considered the memo as an attempt on Watts' part to prevent more thefts from the building. If someone was determined enough to steal a design, the time of day was just a temporary delay for that person. He decided to contact a colleague in New York City who might be able to bring some light into this affair.

"This is Jacob Schreiber, private investigator in Los Angeles. May I speak with Harry Simcoe?" he asked. There was a long wait on the line before the secretary came back to let him know Mr. Simcoe would be right with him.

"Jacob, my friend, haven't seen or heard from you since we left the Marines after the war. I heard you went after what you talked about when we were in the South Pacific. Guess what, I did the same. To what do I owe the honor of your call?" said the eastern gumshoe.

"I have a case I'm working on which requires some investigating in your neck of the woods. My designer client was robbed of one or more of his designs some months back. Now, look-alike copies are showing up nationwide. New York being the heart of the rag business and you an established PI in the city, I would like to contract your services for some work I believe you can handle." Jacob went on to tell Harry about the case and his gut feeling about Earl Edwards being a strong suspect. "I'll send you a photograph of this Edwards guy by courier today. I'll include a retainer fee and you can bill me the overflow once the case is closed. Does that sound acceptable to you, Harry?"

"Not a problem, my friend. Send me that picture. In the meantime I'll poke around the garment district and see what I can pick up," Harry Simcoe concluded.

Jacob was pleased he had been able to get Harry on the telephone immediately. Here was a guy he could trust because of the relationship they had built during their active duties in the Marines together.

Anne came into the office and told him she had some news on the Libbitt case. "Come on in," he said, "and let's see what you have."

"As you had asked me, I hired Ron Pearson to do some picture taking. He's a former military policeman and the kind of guy who knew exactly what we were after. I have thirty photos here," she said as she spread them on his desk. "Six were taken on Libbitt's yacht in Long Beach. Some of the others are from different motels in San Diego and Santa Barbara. There are different women with him, as you can see. I paid Ron and told him we would use his services again."

"Very good work, Anne. You could type the report with all the dates so that we can turn this over to Joan Libbitt. You have a copy of the photos for our file, good. Maybe you could call this Ron Pearson and have him come up here tomorrow if he's available. I could use him on the Watts case," Jacob concluded. "I need to send a photograph of Earl Edwards by courier to Harry Simcoe in New York City. Would you include a check for one thousand dollars with it? I talked to him earlier, he knows what to look for."

Jacob went back to his problem solving. He had a habit of placing

THE BOOKIE

down on paper the different names involved in a case and drew lines interconnecting his characters. Doing that, he made up two or sometimes three different scenarios using the same characters. One of the scenarios always made more sense and he usually went with his gut feeling. Paluka was in jail and obviously not able to conduct business. His place of business had been torched and burned to the ground, taking away any evidence that may have been there. If Jack Paluka got out of jail any time soon he could always set up a new business address. Walking on eggshells was what Jacob had to do for now. There were still some pieces of the puzzle missing and those pieces were most likely the ones that could bring light in this dark tunnel.

What disturbed Jacob the most in the killing of the bookie was where the body had been left. He kept thinking, *why my office?* He was neither a gambler nor a drug user, but still was targeted by whoever did Louis Billings in. No doubt in his mind, Padilla's boys had done the killing, but Black Jack Tony had not ordered it. Someone with lots of money decided for an unknown reason to do away with Louis 'The Snake.'

A knock on the door took him out of his intense concentration. "Come in, Anne," he said.

Anne said, "You have two visitors anxious to talk to you. Would you like me to bring the ladies in right away?"

Jacob frowned a bit but wondered who it could be. "Do the ladies have names?" he asked casually.

"Yes," Anne replied, "the beautiful one is called Lorraine and the gorgeous one, Colette."

The gumshoe stood up to greet the women with a smile and a gentle handshake. "Hi, Lorraine. Nice to meet you, Colette. Don't mind the mess on my desk. I find my way much easier this way. Crime investigation can be time consuming if one does not have enough information to follow-up on," Jacob said.

Lorraine said, "We were shopping close by and I took a chance to bring my sister to meet you, hoping you would not be too busy. Colette is staying with us for two, if not three weeks. She wants to look for a job while she's here. Maybe she'll get lucky and find something real quick."

"What kind of work are you looking for?" Jacob asked Colette.

"I'm a lawyer, Mr. Schreiber. I see there are a number of law offices in this building and most likely in the vicinity. I'm a general law practitioner, but with a specialty in civil litigation. I have handled a couple of criminal cases and honestly prefer the civil side of things."

"Lorraine had not mentioned you were an attorney. I do have a couple of friends who have law firms and know of a handful of other good firms. If you need my help, I'll be happy to make a few contacts for you or at least open a door or two," said a smiling Jacob. "Could I take you both to an afternoon cup of coffee, or did you have other plans?"

"I think we'll take a rain check as they say in baseball," Lorraine said with a grin. "We, that is I, just wanted Colette to meet you privately instead of in front of all the parents tomorrow night," said a happy, nervous, jittery Lorraine. Both women got up to leave the office.

"You are welcome at anytime," Jacob said. "See you both tomorrow," he concluded. Jacob sat behind his desk, reliving the short visit. He felt a strong attachment to Lorraine and was pleased she had brought her sister to meet him in his working environment. He was looking forward to a weekend in La Jolla with this beautiful woman. Thanks to the visiting sister, it was going to happen sooner than later. *However cruel life is, some moments can be energizing,* he thought. If only the energy could be divided equally between work and play. The telephone rang and he heard Anne telling the caller to hold on for a moment.

"Bill Watts is on the line for you, Jacob, it sounds urgent." Anne stated.

"Mr. Watts, I was just thinking about you and your business. What can I do for you right now?" Jacob asked.

"Earl called me about an hour ago. He said he would be coming to Los Angeles to spend the weekend. You did ask me to let you know if he called. If he doesn't know by now about the investigation, I will have to tell him, don't you think, Mr. Schreiber?" said the designer. Jacob replied, "Absolutely, Mr. Watts. I know he has talked to a couple of your employees and is aware of the restrictions you implemented at your workshop. I don't know yet if Mr. Edwards is involved in the disappearance of your designs but keeping a close eye on him wouldn't hurt. Did he say why he was flying to LA on such short notice?"

Watts answered, "He just said he was coming for a visit. Needed to get away from Dallas and his father is what he actually said. I told him I was very busy with my upcoming fashion show and would not have much time to spend with him. Earl did not seem to mind, so I left it at that."

In retrospect, Jacob remembered asking Bill Watts to inform him about any conversation with Earl. *This young Edwards is a shrewd operator*, Jacob thought. *Making sure Watts knows about his coming to LA would be the right approach if he were involved in the thefts of Watts Enterprises designs. It would be interesting to find out from Harry Simcoe in New York City if this same Earl Edwards has been seen around with top designers. Now why would the son of a Texas oil millionaire want to involve himself with organized crime characters? They would certainly use him as a scapegoat if the need arises, and without blinking an eye.*

Jacob left everything on his desk, walked out and told his secretary he would only be back tomorrow morning at his usual time. While doing his thinking and laying out the puzzle, a name popped in his mind. Laverne Holiday was a war widow he had helped with what he classified a major man problem. He also recalled that he had not charged her anything. As he got in his car driving out of the parking lot, he took the direction indicating the Pasadena freeway. Laverne lived almost at the very top of Pasadena. She had worked in the garment district of Los Angeles. He remembered some of the stories she told him about making garments from modified patterns. Now this woman could certainly bring some answers to many of his questions. He didn't know why right now but maybe, just maybe this

Laverne could be of help.

The Pasadena freeway was always a pain to travel because all the major Los Angeles commercial traffic used it to connect from the valley to downtown. It was almost supper time when he got to Miss Holiday's place. Her old car was parked out front. A dog was laid out on the front lawn, or what used to be a grass cover.

When Jacob approached the walk to the front steps, the old dog got up and came over to sniff him. He couldn't tell what breed he was, most likely a Heinz '57 variety. Even before he reached the top step the door swung open and Laverne, all her 200 pounds, said in a loud voice, "Mr. Schreiber, is that you?"

"It is, Laverne," Jacob said. "I was in the vicinity and thought I would stop by to say hello. It's been quite some time since we last met. How have you been? Those guys not bothering you I hope," the gumshoe concluded.

"Not at all," Laverne said. "Let me get you a cold beer and we can sit on the porch here in the shade where it's cool."

When Laverne returned Jacob said, "Did you not tell me some time ago you had worked in the rag business in downtown LA?"

"That I did, Mr. Schreiber. It was more of a sweatshop atmosphere than a regular manufacturing place. A Mexican who had a couple of tough Negro women as supervisors operated it. Most of the forty or fifty woman working in the warehouse was Mexicans, only five of us were Negroes. It didn't take Einstein to figure out this operation was not fully legitimate. Would you like me to tell you about the two years I spent there?"

"Why don't you do that, Laverne; it sounds very interesting."

CHAPTER TWENTY-ONE...

Jacob was back from a wonderful weekend spent with Lorraine. The two had become lovers and he was happy about it. They both knew it was bound to happen. How it would be felt by both was the big question. As his thoughts were traveling through his mind, Anne came in.

"Good morning, Jacob," she said. "Did you have a nice time in La Jolla?" Anne asked with a smile on her face.

"Yes, we both did. The boating was as excellent as the weather. The food fabulous and the company exceptional," he concluded. "Anything else you would like to know will not be said by yours truly. Would you find out from Ron Pearson if the photographs he took at Watts Enterprises are ready? I have a funny feeling about the whole thing. I just cannot seem to put my finger on what's nagging at me. The mail just came in, let me know if there's something of interest before I go to my meeting in Santa Monica."

Anne came rushing back in. "Look at this, Jacob. You are invited to a wedding in Santa Monica, a month from today. Who is this Alexander Fitzsimmons? Never heard you mention the name before."

Jacob looked at the invitation and said, "This is an old buddy from the Marines. Some time ago I ran into him on the Santa Monica Pier, just forgot to mention it with all that was happening around here. I'm going to have to do some searching for an appropriate wedding present, don't you think?"

Now what could two artistic people who have been together for some time need that would be practical? Jacob would have to rely on both his secretary's judgement and Lorraine's too.

Anne informed her boss that Lieutenant Jones was on the telephone.

"You're up bright and early for a civil servant," the gumshoe said with a smile in his voice. "What did you have in mind for me today, my friend?" he asked.

"Jacob, I stumbled across something that you may find interesting. You mentioned to me you were investigating a possible ring of industrial espionage last time we had coffee together. If you're free at lunchtime I would like to have a talk with you, preferably somewhere we don't have to be concerned about being overheard. What do you say?" concluded the detective.

Jacob answered, "How about meeting at Jim Lee's restaurant in Chinatown? It's about the best one I can think of aside from the country club. Okay, see you in Chinatown at 2 o'clock."

The private eye wondered what could his friend have stumbled across that would somehow connect with the case he was working on now. Sometimes the lieutenant was careful not to appear to be too cozy with Jacob when other members of the LAPD were around. The whole homicide division knew Schreiber and respected him. Some had either been in the Marines or Navy during the war and for whatever reason felt a bond with a guy who had been there himself.

While in Santa Monica, Jacob stopped by his friend's store to let him know he had received the wedding invitation and would be there with a companion. Alexander was pleased to see his wartime friend would be at the wedding. He only had one brother who was a priest back East.

Jacob went to his favorite meeting place, the pier where one could talk freely without fear of being overheard. He was meeting with Paul, the security man from Watts Industries. Some things he wanted to tell the gumshoe out of earshot of employees, especially Mario the shop foreman.

Paul said, "You know ,Mr. Schreiber, there has been some funny stuff going on at the shop for a few months. I remember it was about eight or nine months ago when late one evening Mr. Earl wanted to be let in. If I recall right it was around 10 PM. I found this unusual, but since I had seen him many times before with Mr. Watts, I didn't think he would be doing anything criminal. Besides, he always carried one of those big awkward leather, what do you call them, oh yeah... portfolios. Over a period of several months, the same thing went on and at times Mario was with Mr. Earl. It was not my job to ask them what they were doing in the work area late at night. Sometimes Mr. Earl volunteered that they had a special project going on."

Jacob asked, "Did you ever see anyone else but Mario and Watts with Earl over that long period of time?"

"No, Mr. Schreiber, it was always Mario or Mr. Watts who came in with Mr. Earl. I must tell you that one night about three months ago when Mr. Earl came in, he arrived in a limousine. All the time, about half an hour, he was in the shop, the limo waited outside. When I unlocked the door to let him out, I noticed there was someone sitting inside who had waited for him, but I could not tell who it was. From the laughter I heard I'm sure there was more than one person hiding in there."

Paul did not have any more information to give away. Jacob asked him to keep their meeting confidential. "No use in alarming anyone at this time since we don't really know what happened," he said.

After doing some window shopping in Santa Monica, Jacob headed for Chinatown for his lunch date with Lieutenant Jones. There were many new businesses opening along the way. Now that the war was over, the whole aerospace industry had come to a standstill. Some eighty percent of the workers were laid off and left greater LA in droves. Newly arrived immigrants opened small businesses and generated a welcome boost to the lagging economy. Jacob was thinking about that, and the crime factor these dramatic changes always bring. He was also going through the information Paul, the security guy, had given him. Strange that Watts had not told him about Earl having free access to the workshop. There had to be a clue somewhere, he just was not seeing it yet!

"You found your way here without a map," Jacob teased his friend. "Let's go in and get a special table from Jim Lee. He's always happy to see us come back to his restaurant."

They were seated in a small private dining enclosure where no one would disturb them. The gumshoe said, "Do you think these rooms were used by opium smokers at one time, Bill?"

The lieutenant answered, "I have no doubt they still are. The Chinese people do things much differently than we Westerners do. They are not as exuberant and prefer quiet surroundings. Only when they cannot see a solution to the problem they're facing do they ask for help. Usually by that time it's almost always too late."

There was a silent pause before the food was ordered and then Bill Jones began telling his friend why he had called him. "Just about three weeks ago," he began, "a shipment was being unloaded at the marine terminals in Long Beach. The ship was registered in Hong Kong. Except for the captain and a handful of officers (they were British), the rest of the crew was Chinese. On the dock were three tractor-trailers waiting to be loaded. Everything they loaded on those trucks was a garment and, according to the bills of lading, was to be delivered to major stores in Los Angeles, Phoenix and San Francisco. So far this does not sound unusual, does it, Jacob?"

"Not that I can see, Lieutenant. Nothing out of the ordinary unless you are looking at the manufacturing side of things," Jacob answered.

Bill Jones went on, "One of my investigators who was looking for information concerning another case got a surprise. The ship in question had not just arrived directly from Hong Kong but rather from the East coast of the United States. He also recognized from old mug shots a couple of organized crime goons from the Cartolli family out of New Jersey. Now why would all that have any bearing on what you are working on now? Very simple, in taking a closer look at the paperwork he stumbled across the name of Earl Edwards. Now that brings your eyebrows up, my friend. This officer had previously worked on the vice squad and was familiar with the Edwards name. Again, I say as I said before, why would the son of a super rich Texas oil man have his name mixed with garment shipments from the East coast? More tingling is the way they shipped it. Trying to make it look as if it came from China. The same investigator watched as a car arrived and Mr. Edwards came out to greet one of the Mafia guys. Now if that doesn't take the cake, what

THE BOOKIE

does?"

Jacob was almost speechless. His mind was almost racing at the speed of light. "You should have been a writer, Lieutenant. Fantastic story you just told me, and you know what, it's all starting to make sense. I have the feeling I'm being used to cover up something. The deeper I get into this, the further away I am from the source. Somehow, I have the feeling that all of this is in a way related to Louis Billings' death. Don't you think so?"

Bill Jones answered, "It's like a spider web, every strand leads to the center. I don't see the connection yet between garment shipments and the killing of Louis 'The Snake' Billings. However, I have been proven wrong before. This won't be the last time."

Jacob said, "Don't feel bad, Bill, I don't have the solution yet either. There are still some pieces of the puzzle missing, and when I find them, you'll be the first one to know. Interesting what you just told me. In a day or two, our Mr. Earl Edwards is supposed to call me. There are many questions I want to ask this young man. I'm waiting to hear from a PI I hired in New York City. I sent him a photograph of Edwards and he was going to poke around the garment district for me. Are criminals getting more sophisticated, or are we just behind the times here?"

Bill Jones said, "I asked you before to join the LAPD and work with me. You know we would make a great team. I know, I know, there isn't enough money to drag you over. Moreover, you don't like restrictions or anyone telling you what to do. Too bad," Jones continued with a smile, "we could have this case wrapped up in no time."

Jacob said, "The lunch is on me since you think I make more money than you do. It's really not a question of money, Bill. I just don't want to follow orders as I did in the Marines. One experience, one war was enough for me. In a way I'm a free soul, and I would certainly like to stay that way."

The gumshoe thanked his friend for the new information and they parted company. On his way back to the office, he tried to fit the missing puzzle pieces to no avail. When he turned in the parking lot behind his office building, his instinct immediately told him to be on the lookout. Just as he was getting out of the car, he heard a car engine roar and hit the pavement. Lucky for him, the bullets went flying over his head. He started firing back and this time got both rear tires of the fleeing car. Two men jumped out, ran a few feet and right into a waiting car that sped away before Jacob could get closer.

Someone wants me out of the way, he thought. He ran up the steps to his office and at the same time holstered his .45 out of the way.

Anne did not have time to say anything to him; he blurted out, "Call Lieutenant Jones immediately, it's urgent. Somebody just shot at me again. I wish I knew what I'm doing right to scare them so much."

"Lieutenant, guess what, no sooner do I arrive at my office parking space that someone tried to plug holes in me again. I got the two rear tires of the car, but they had another one waiting and got away. You could send your men to investigate and remove what I think is a stolen car. Thanks, Bill, let's have lunch again soon, it seems to create excitement."

Anne walked in his office and said, "You have a knack at attracting bullets, luckily none hit you. Do you have any idea who's behind this, Jacob?"

"My dear secretary, it's all part of a day's work. I just wish it did not happen every day. This kind of stuff ruins my clothing," he said with a smile. You see, I tore a hole at the knee level on the right pant leg. If whoever is behind these attacks was serious about doing me in, he would have done so long ago. I think they want me to be scared away. It won't work."

CHAPTER TWENTY-TWO...

Lieutenant Jones could not believe how lucky his friend Jacob Schreiber had been recently. Two attempts on his life had been made, and twice he escaped injuries. This would not go on forever. Scare tactics, his friend had said. Since Tony Padilla had been indicted on federal charges, a gang war was creeping up. Those wanting to take over the control of organized crime in southern California would stop at nothing to achieve their goal. First they began by burning down Jack Paluka's pawnshop building, thinking he would burn with it too. A few hours before the torching, Paluka had been arrested by the FBI and charged as an accessory in the theft of military weapons. None of the nine people arrested in that indictment would be granted bail. The drug distribution market was up for grabs as well as the gambling, prostitution, loan sharking and extortion sector. A New York family friendly to the Padilla clan had tried a fast move without success. Five of their members were eliminated when a limo they were going to drive away in, blew up. The going was rough, but it shouldn't touch a local PI like Schreiber. The car used on the latest attack on the gumshoe had been reported stolen as previously thought.

The only interesting development the lieutenant had was connected to Jacob's current investigation on industrial espionage. For some reason, the name of Louis Billings kept coming up. A paper trail had been found linking a group of Mafia enforcers from back East to the local bookie. This Louis sure had his hands in everything from horse betting to illegal sales of stolen military weapons and now to the garment industry. There could be a small possibility Jacob's wish of wanting to know why The Snake's body was dumped in his office may be solved. It was still a remote possibility but a possibility nonetheless.

As his thoughts were racing through his head, the telephone rang.

"Jones here," he answered. "Good morning, Jacob, this must be mental telepathy, I was just thinking about you and how you manage to have more lives than a cat. What's on your mind today?" asked the detective.

Jacob said, "Let me tell you, Lieutenant, this industrial espionage case is getting bigger by the minute. Just got a call from Harry Simcoe, a New York PI I hired last week. He just told me about Earl Edwards' wide range of friends, from the ordinary waiter to the Broadway actor, on to the designer group and a touch of Mafia cronies to finish the circle. According to the findings of my friend Harry, Mr. Earl is very well known and respected in the New York garment district. What your investigator stumbled across at the Long Beach docks may be more significant than I originally thought. Someone with direct access to designers' workshops is stealing without actually taking anything away from these shops. Right now it boggles the mind, but I'm getting closer to putting the mechanics of all this together. Got time for coffee this morning? How about my place? Good, I'll see you in forty-five minutes."

Lieutenant Jones was looking forward to his talk with Jacob. Now he could bring up Louis Billings' name again. This time he had concrete evidence the bookie had also been involved in the movement of copied garments across the nation. Someone had said to him that the money generated in the 'rag' business was more than the federal budget.

"Anne, do you think you could get us all some coffee and doughnuts from the corner store? Take some money out of the petty cash box. Well, my friend, it has been a busy time with all the car blow-ups, bodies being dumped everywhere, and shoot outs in public parking lots in full daylight. The LAPD must be out of overtime money. So, you do have a gang war on your hands. As long as it doesn't affect the public, it serves as a process of elimination. Too many scumbags around, cleaning up the streets won't hurt. From the sound of your voice this morning I have the feeling you want to tell me a war story or two."

"Not really, Jacob," said the lieutenant. "I believe we are getting

THE BOOKIE

closer to solving the mystery of the dead body left in your office." As the detective finished his sentence, Jacob's eyebrows perked up.

"Now, Lieutenant, what would make you say such a thing? Found any new evidence to back up your statement?" Jacob said.

"It's not complete yet, but getting closer," the detective said. "I have found some paper trail that links Louis 'The Snake' to shipments of garments across the country."

"Wow, that puts another twist to the 'rag' saga. On your paper trail, does Earl Edwards' name come up too?" Jacob asked.

"Not in what I have found so far, Jacob. Tony Padilla's name was there and some other names, which I'm sure are or were associates of Padilla. It also identifies the garment style, meaning which designer originally produced it. Mind you, these are all copies of somebody else's originals and I have a feeling it won't be easy to prove that they are stolen copies. Who would have thought that a regular off-the-street bookie like Louis 'The Snake' would have had such contacts? Think about it, Jacob, the arms deals with African countries and now this garment saga, no wonder someone wanted to eliminate Louis. He must have done or said something to the wrong person."

"I know what you're thinking, Lieutenant. Still it does not give me an answer as to why his body was dumped on my lap. Maybe I should forget about it, like most people would do, but I cannot. Do you think Padilla knows the answer I'm searching for?"

"No, Jacob, Padilla doesn't care what happens to you. Remember that you are the source of all bad things that are happening to him right now. He was arrested in front of your office building while one of his men was trying or supposedly trying to intimidate you. He felt certain Louis had left you the information he was after. This may be the reason why someone is taking pot shots at you. Maybe the rival gangs will get to who is left from Padilla's stable before they get to you. This is a dangerous time for you, Jacob. You cannot go to the press and say, 'I don't have any information regarding stolen military weapons'. For whatever reason he had, Louis placed you in a bind. Maybe he wanted to get revenge on you for investigating his social life and reporting some of it back to his wife. I personally think he singled you out because he had no other avenue that a mobster like Padilla would believe."

"Whichever way you put it, Lieutenant, I'm still being used for target practice, and I don't like it. I feel as if I'm living in the old west where a man had to carry his gun and be ready for a shootout at the blink of an eye. I know you've been wanting to close this case since the Padilla gang is in jail. Somehow, new information keeps creeping up on you. We both know the mob wanted the list of contacts Louis had. I just got lucky and found it first. Again, this all happened after the bookie's demise, why me? The only contacts I had with Louis before that was during my tailing him for divorce purposes, and I never spoke to him then or after. There is another connection somewhere we are not making. Louis had contacts locally, statewide, in New York, New Jersey, the Middle East, Eastern Europe and Africa. For a small-time operator he was sure playing on a large field."

"That is the point, Jacob. How does a small time bookie acquire so much power and yet remain relatively unknown? Maybe he took some acting lessons in Hollywood. All joking aside, my friend, I have to agree with you that there has to be a missing link here. I wonder if a friendly meeting with Special Agent Trickten would be helpful. What do you think, Jacob?"

"I'm not so sure about the FBI giving us any cooperation right now. Don't forget they have their goat locked up and secured. For them to come forward with any information that may help us unwind a domestic problem, the incentive would have to be big. I can't think of anything more you or I could give them right now. Unless, and let me say that very carefully, there is a definite connection between the movement of illegal drugs, stolen military weapons and copied designer wear. Does that make any sense to you, Lieutenant?"

"It could be that you're right, Jacob. Neither you nor I have the needed resources to look into such an elaborate international set-up. I wonder how Louis did it. The local stuff he did such as prostitutes and markers was all controlled by Tony Padilla. The stolen arms deal was probably in cooperation with other Mafia families around the country. For an unknown reason Louis had the contacts; they had the work force and the ability to steal the weapons and prepare them for shipment. This operation was bigger than we thought. I wonder why they bumped Louis? It has to be over money. A lot of money like in millions. Maybe the bookie had a secret bank account in Switzerland. That will be very difficult to trace. Gangland-style executions are usually done to send a message to others that might have an idea of cheating the 'family.' It was reported in the local papers, the *New York Times* and the *Chicago Tribune* that a Los Angeles bookie had been murdered Mafia-style." The detective thought for a moment and added, "When Tony Padilla was indicted on the weapons deal, Louis' name and how he died was mentioned. He was also listed as one of Padilla's close associates."

Jacob said, "I'm going to be double careful from now on. I hate to be looking over my shoulder, but if this is what it takes, life has to go on. I have made another contact in Boston concerning the stolen design from Watts Industries. Maybe some different information will come out of there. At least this is what I hope for. Once I have all my sources in, I may be able to place the last pieces of the puzzle together. I guess the DA has given up on the Billings case. In fact, you had given up too just a few days ago. All this new information you're picking up is making your feet itchy, is it not?" the gumshoe concluded.

"Something had to nudge me hard enough to consider looking at the Billings case again. There is so much on my plate I'm falling behind on the rest of my work," Lieutenant Jones said.

There was a knock on the door and Anne said, "Harry Simcoe is on the line for you, Jacob."

"Harry, you must have something new to tell me, I'm all ears," Jacob said. After a few minutes of back and forth conversation he hung up. "Well, Lieutenant, this New York guy has added another twist to our saga. An informer told him that small groups of designers from New York, Boston and Los Angeles have set up a cartel. Would you believe that they steal from each other? They then have sweatshops organized by the Mafia manufacture the stolen designs.

At the same time, these sweatshops use illegal immigrants to do the work. Some of those migrants end up in prostitution rings all over America. Whoever thought of this plan must be taking money in by the millions. The profit sharing has to be well organized, or they may be using a barter system where goods or services are exchanged instead of cash. I still don't understand why Louis was done in," Jacob ended.

The lieutenant said, "You must look at the bigger picture, Jacob. I don't know if the stolen military weapons and the designer goods are connected together. From what you found in his house and briefcase, we know Louis Billings had the contacts for the sale of military weapons and goods. When it comes to the 'rag' business, there is not much there to indicate a connection. Louis Billings was connected to Padilla for his bookie operation and had a big hand in the arms deal. His name does not show up anywhere else other than being in cahoots with known mobsters. You and I have some more digging to do, my friend."

They both decided to keep in touch twice a day either by telephone or physically. Until this whole mystery was solved, Jacob would have to be more alert than he normally was and, at the same time, keep his eyes open for anything out of the ordinary or any strangers in his surroundings. Such is life as a private investigator.

CHAPTER TWENTY-THREE...

The Little League baseball season was ending. School would be starting soon. Jacob's team had reach the finals by winning their last schedule game on a home run by Gerald Buford in the bottom of the ninth inning. Just like the big leagues, the coach had said. The after-the-game celebration was a happy event for everyone concerned.

Lorraine's sister Colette had found work with a prestigious law firm in Hollywood. She was now handling all litigation coming out of the movie studios. Still, she had time to come watch her young nephew play ball. She, although not personally interested, admired the coach. Colette could see the relationship growing between Lorraine and Jacob. Many times she had noticed how patient he was with the kids on the team and the special attention he gave to Gerald. On different occasions during a friendly conversation she had almost brought up the subject of matrimony, but held her tongue. Let the chips fall where they may, she had thought. Moreover, fall they did. Just before the end of the baseball season Jacob had gathered the courage to ask Lorraine if she would at a point in time, soon he meant, consider him to become her husband. She had been a bit surprised, but not totally surprised. She questioned him about the responsibility of being a father image to Gerald. He didn't see a problem in that area. The private eye even said he would legally adopt Gerald if they both agreed. That's how he felt about the boy, just as if he was his own.

Anne, her husband and Colette had thrown a big party once they found out about Jacob and Lorraine's plans. It was a real happy mood all around and an actual wedding date was set for the upcoming Thanksgiving.

Jacob was quietly going through his notes on both the Billings case and the Watts Enterprises one. He felt the two incidents, although they appeared to be so far apart, were closely interconnected. How they were, he did not have his finger on it yet, but knew it would soon blow up in his face. As he sat there thinking about every possible angle, his secretary knocked on his door.

"Come in, Anne," he said. "Once I'm done with this telephone call you're just about to tell me about, I would like you to come back in here and study this plan I laid out. I need your opinion. I just may be going in the wrong direction here. Mr. Edwards senior is on the telephone, thank you."

"Mr. Edwards, what brings you to my side of the world today?" Jacob asked the rich oilman from Texas.

"I have a problem I would like to discuss with you. It concerns my son Earl. I'm planning on coming to Los Angeles in the next day or two. Would you have some time to see me on short notice, Mr. Schreiber?" Leon Edwards asked.

"As long as you let me know when and where you want to meet, I'll be glad to do so, Mr. Edwards." After he put the telephone down, Jacob's mind started to race, trying to figure out what this millionaire with an oddball son, if not a renegade son, would want to talk about. *Interesting that he should call at this time of the game*, he was thinking just as Anne came back in his office.

"You said, Mr. Investigator, that you wanted me to look at your funny drawings here. Let's have them," she said. Jacob carried his papers to the round table where Anne could sit down and look at the plan her boss had put together. It looked more like the drawing of a pyramid with names all over. She had been looking at it for about fifteen minutes when the telephone rang. She was just in the process of getting up when Jacob motioned he would answer it.

"Schreiber investigation," Jacob here. "Well, Lieutenant, no, Anne is not on strike, holiday or gone for the day. In fact, she's doing some thinking at this time. Yes, she's thinking for me since my brains are in a dormant state. Oh, I see. Well, we could meet when it's convenient for you, my friend," the gumshoe said. "Let's meet on Sunset Place; we could have a hot dog or hamburger and a soft drink. Good, I'll see you there in about forty-five minutes," Jacob concluded.

THE BOOKIE

Jacob said to Anne, "Do you find my puzzle interesting? Is it confusing, or does it make sense to you?" he said.

Anne replied, "I can almost see where you're going with this. First let me say that for whatever reason you have in mind, you have connected the Louis Billings murder to the illegal military weapons theft and the designer saga as you call it. Am I on the right track so far, boss?"

"No doubt you are, but give me more of your talented analysis," Jacob said.

"There is something missing here. Not only a name but how come you don't have anything related to drug trafficking? This really was one of the major sides of Tony Padilla's operation. Everything else is in there but the drug dealings and the pushers etc. Is there a special reason for you to leave that out? Don't you think that moving garments from east to west, north and south, would be the perfect way to move shipments of cocaine and heroin with a very slight risk of being caught?" Anne concluded.

"I told you before, Anne, you should get yourself a law degree. With your mind, you would become the first female DA in Los Angeles. It's interesting you should bring up the drug business. Sometimes one cannot see the forest for the trees and this is exactly what happened to me. I don't know what I would do without you. Lieutenant Jones had previously said to me that one of his men had been keeping an eye on arrivals in Long Beach. He was looking for ships from the Far East or the Mediterranean. You may have come up with part of the answer I'm looking for. I was so absorbed by the military weapons and the industrial espionage that I totally forgot about the drugs. Jones and I are getting together for a quick lunch. I'll come back to my discussion with you when I return. Thanks, Anne, you've been a great help," Jacob concluded.

His thinking machine was now working on full throttle. Padilla and the Mafia were the main players in the drug business. The minor players could possibly include Louis Billings as well as Earl Edwards. Then he thought about the letter he had received from Terry Downs where drugs were mentioned along with conversations he had heard on selling military weapons to African countries. Now where did he put this letter? He looked in all the drawers of his desk but could not find it. He walked to the front office and asked Anne if she had a file under the name of Terry Downs. When she answered negatively, he went to the wall safe and pulled out a large envelope, which he knew contained papers he had found at Louis Billings' house. Back at his desk, he dumped the content of the envelope and there it was, a regular white letter size envelope addressed to him. He opened it and started to read the contents again. There it was in plain bold writing, a list of five names associated with drug trafficking. The first three names belonged to Padilla, Paluka and Billings. The fourth name he didn't know immediately, but the last name on the list got his attention. Earl Edwards' name associated with undesirable characters. This young man sure had his hands in every crooked deal one could think of. Why would the son of a rich Texan, who happened to be an only child, want to have his name associated with Tony Padilla, the godfather of organized crime in southern California? The more he thought about this, the more the association between the shipment of garments and cocaine together became plausible.

"Hope you haven't been waiting too long, Lieutenant," Jacob said as he sat with Detective Jones. "Anything special on your mind, or did you just want to get away from the office? I have an angle I'm going to try on you and see if it helps us solve the problem we have." Jacob told his friend about the possible connection between the garment shipments and the drug distribution. "I know it sounds far-fetched but your man was looking for shipments of cocaine. It's possible that the drugs came with the garments from the East coast instead of being aboard a ship from the Far East or the Mediterranean. It could be easy to have loads of cocaine in shoe boxes, for example. I know I have a suspicious mind, but think of it, Lieutenant. How simple it would be to pack cocaine or heroin in shoe boxes instead of shoes? The boxes are then packed in a larger container for shipment. Does that make any sense at all?"

The lieutenant said, "I think sometimes you must have been a magician in your previous life. This is not the first time you hit the nail on the head. Let me explain why, Jacob." Jones told his friend about the box his detective found yesterday in a Long Beach warehouse. "My two-man crew had been snooping in there for many weeks without success and yesterday he stumbled across a large carton damaged in the handling. Inside the carton were empty shoe boxes, except for one where the content had been spilled. His partner told him it was cocaine in its purest form. Nothing else was in the carton and no consignment address could be found. The warehouse manager told him he was not aware it was even there and whom it could belong to. He told my men that the garment containers had been picked up by a local LA trucking company, the same one who picked up the same kind of shipments before. Where they went or who had ordered them originally, the bill of lading did not show that, the manager said. Are you sure you're not a mind reader, Jacob? You seem to have the ability to come up with facts that only a person who has been there or been told about it would know," concluded the detective.

"It's really not that complicated, Lieutenant, I just put two and two together and come up with an answer. I may not have the proper names but getting my puzzles to work is not a problem. Remember when you asked me about Terry Downs some time back? You wondered if he was a client of mine because my name and address had been found in his pockets. Well, I don't know if I told you this, but he had written me a letter before he died. The man wanted to get out of the bookie business because he was afraid for his life. He said that dealing with Louis was not difficult but Jack Paluka was a problem for him. Downs said he feared that man. He did not say why he was afraid of Paluka, just that he was afraid. In his dealing with Louis 'The Snake' he saw many things and overheard some conversations that were the basis of his fears. These were about military weapons being stolen from different armed forces establishments across the nation. He also heard Louis talk on the telephone with someone about designer garments, cocaine and whatever. This man's fears came true. He was murdered because he knew or had heard too much. His letter had a list of five names, here they are," Jacob said.

The lieutenant took the list from Jacob's hand and stared at it briefly. "I know four of these names but haven't got a clue about the fourth one down. It sounds like an Arab or could even be an African name. Do you know who the name belongs to Jacob?" Bill Jones asked.

"No, Lieutenant, I know the four other names, but that fifth one has me stymied. It could be one of their overseas contacts. Don't you find it out of place for Earl Edwards' name to be there? By the way, his father called me from Dallas today. He's coming out here in a day or two and wants to talk to me about his son's acquaintances. This should be a very interesting conversation. Coming back to Earl, I first found out the young man is a homosexual and most likely a male prostitute. Then I find him involved in stealing original designs for mass manufacturing. Along the way, his name shows up alongside that of Louis Billings, Jack Paluka and Tony Padilla. Now, this is not the kind of company you have at a high school prom or the kind you invite home to meet your parents. That may sound unlikely to you but when you trace Earl Edwards' comings and goings, you find him strictly in the company of well-to-do men. Most of the men are successful designers or store owners. Some of the men I found are married and instead of having a mistress, they have sex with another male, kinky people they are, wouldn't you say? The potential for extortion is enormous in these cases. The fear of being exposed will make these individuals do things they would not normally do. Like trafficking in cocaine or heroin. They become ideal targets for the likes of Tony Padilla and other mafiosos. The fear of being physically hurt and exposed publicly is greater in these men than the fear of being caught by the police. I don't know how Earl Edwards became the sort of go between for the mob, but that is exactly what he is, Lieutenant," Jacob concluded.

"You have a strong point there, Jacob. Let's talk about it some more after your meeting with Edwards senior."

CHAPTER TWENTY-FOUR...

Jacob did not know what to expect from Leon Edwards. The original retainer the oilman had given him still had half of its value left. Early this morning he had received a call from Edwards' secretary informing him of Leon's arrival in Los Angeles. The old man had requested an audience at 10 o'clock. It was nine-thirty and the private investigator was going through his drawn plan again. Lieutenant Jones had told Jacob earlier in the morning about the shooting at one of Padilla's nightclub in the early hours of the morning. The bartender said that around three in the morning five patrons were quietly seating at a center table sipping wine. The entertainment was over and most of the regular customers had left, except for five individuals who belonged to the Padilla family group. Then all of a sudden all hell broke loose. Four guys entered through the front door carrying machine guns. The bartender said he jumped through the escape trap he had behind the bar. Some ten to fifteen minutes later when he didn't hear anymore shooting, he climbed back into the bar and surveyed the damage. There were six dead bodies on the floor. The five mentioned as belonging to the Padilla group and one from a rival gang. The internal war was intensifying with no let up in sight. All this information the lieutenant had said was to inform Jacob about a piece of paper found in the pocket of one of the dead men. It said, 'Kill the gumshoe and I'll have five thousand dollars in cash for you, TP.' It sure looked like Black Jack Tony wanted to get rid of Schreiber the investigator. So far, the internal war had prevented anyone from fulfilling their former boss' wishes. Thirty-two men from the Padilla ranks had been eliminated. Many others had already joined forces with the new boss, Vito Profacini, a Sicilian with strong New York ties.

The rumors were flying that Profacini had sent an army of two hundred men to assure the takeover of Padilla's business interest. In their own little world there were no negotiations when one group decided to take over a territory formally controlled by another group. Assassinations were the rule of the day. You either joined or were eliminated. In a sort of way, this was good for Jacob. Since the new gang did not have a beef with him, they would leave him alone. No need to attract attention to yourself when you're new in the neighborhood. Most people don't understand a thing about these murders. In the underworld, they serve as a process of elimination. The stronger arm wins the election and becomes the new don, one that the subordinates learn to fear and obey without questioning. A knock on his door brought him back to reality. Anne informed him Leon Edwards had arrived.

Jacob got up to great the old man. "Good morning, Mr. Edwards, hope you had a pleasant flight," he said to initiate the conversation. After getting coffees and doughnuts, they got down to the oilman's reasons for being here.

Leon Edwards said, "What I want to talk over with you, Mr. Schreiber, is of the upmost sensitivity. I would want our conversation and what I'm about to reveal to you to stay between us, if it's agreeable with you?"

"I don't see why not, Mr. Edwards. I'm like a lawyer, what you say to me is privileged information. By the way, I would prefer if you call me Jacob, and may I call you Leon?"

"That's very friendly of you, Jacob, I agree to that. Just give me a moment to sort my thoughts out so that I can tell you in the proper sequence."

Jacob excused himself for a moment and left Edwards alone. He asked Anne to take all telephone messages while Leon Jones was here. Of course, there is always the exception of an emergency and she would know what to do then.

Leon Edwards began, "You may already know that my son Earl is involved in drug trafficking. He's also involved in stealing original drawings from designers. Worst of all I recently found out he is a male prostitute in great demand. Furthermore, he is associated with known criminals of the worst kind. How do I know all this? First, let me show you and then let me tell you. In this briefcase," he said as he opened it, "I found books with names and telephone numbers. Bank books with large sums of money in his name. Money that I did not give him. For your information, I have been giving him a yearly allowance of $50K a year, until four days ago that is. I cancelled that allowance and changed my will. I haven't confronted him yet, but intend to do so within the next week. I know there is a whole lot more Earl has been involved in and I'm afraid to find out. You, as a private investigator, have ways and sources which allow you to find things faster than I would. Here's a check for $50,000. I want you to find all you can about my son's activity and put it in a report for me. Don't be afraid to tell me the truth. I have finally come to accept that my son does not deserve my kindness. Now to what I heard. The Dallas Chief of Police and I go back to high school days together. We have been friends since our early teens. A week ago he came to me with a somber attitude as if he was almost afraid to talk to me. When he finally opened up, he told me about Earl being a male prostitute for the Mafia. His encounters are strictly with rich men who are then extorted for money or products. This is the most despicable thing I had ever heard about my son. I am hurt, Jacob, deeply hurt. I am also realistic and have to bring an end to my emotions. Don't get me wrong, I don't want to end my life. What I want to end is my association with Earl. I have voted him off the board of directors of my oil company and replaced him with one of my cousins. My friend also told me that Earl could himself be involved in some extortion, even murder. This whole thing really pains me to no end, Jacob. Fortunately for him his mother died of cancer two years ago and does not have to find out how bad our son turned out to be. Would you do a full investigation and report for me? I know my check is quite more than what you would actually charge, but I need this report fast, so it's worth it to me," concluded a downhearted father.

"I don't know what to say, Leon. I have been finding out things about Earl almost on a daily basis. His association with Tony Padilla is the worst move he could have made. He also has a drug addiction you may not know about and there lies the reason for his Mafia association. Knowing what Padilla is like, I know fear of death or torture was placed on your son if he didn't comply with Tony's demands. I'll have a report ready for you in two days and send it by courier to your office. I don't think what I will say in my report will ease your pain, Leon, but if I can in some way make you feel somewhat better, I'll try to do so." Jacob got up to escort Leon Edwards to the door where his chauffeur was waiting.

"Anne, could you bring me the file on Edwards?" Jacob asked as he was walking back to his office. When his secretary placed the file on his desk, he handed her the check from Edwards to be deposited. As she looked at it, she let out a long surprised whistle.

Jacob picked up the telephone and called his friend Lieutenant Jones. He wanted to meet with him as soon as possible to discuss the Edwards case. Maybe they could end Earl Edwards' extra social activities if a serious charge could be laid on him. Bill Jones agreed to meet him at the Wilshire Country Club for lunch.

"Anne, could you see if you can get Paul Trickten on the telephone?" Jacob asked.

"Good morning, Paul, this is Jacob Schreiber. I would like to meet with you either late today or early tomorrow morning if you can. I have something which may be of interest to you regarding cocaine distribution. Tomorrow morning 8 o'clock at the Santa Monica Pier, sounds good to me."

Jacob picked up his notes and placed them in his middle drawer before leaving for the country club. As he was driving in the parking lot, he noticed an LAPD patrol car dropping off the lieutenant. *Good timing*, he said to himself.

"Well, Jacob, how did your conversation with Edwards senior go? Did he bring something new, or was he just feeling out what you know?" the lieutenant asked.

Jacob answered, "Neither, my friend. This man found out about his son's activities and is quite upset at the whole situation. So much so that he cut off the funds he was supplying him, voted him off his board of directors and wrote a new will, leaving Earl out of it. Leon Edwards is devastated by what his son has done. A school friend who

THE BOOKIE

is now the Dallas Chief of Police painted a very dark picture for the grieving father. He talked about male prostitution, thefts of original designs and extortion. What he was not aware of is the drug habit his son has as well as his hand in the whole distribution of cocaine nationwide," Jacob concluded. "Tomorrow morning I'm meeting with Paul Trickten at the Santa Monica Pier, would you like to join us? I think that we all have an interest in young Mr. Edwards and this meeting should be revealing."

"There is no reason for me not to be there," the lieutenant said. "I for one would like to see a stop to the drug trafficking that is being done through the port of Long Beach and using the garment shipments as a cover-up. This is going to hurt many people who had not intended to be involved in drugs. The association they made with Earl Edwards is going to cost them more than they could ever imagine. Because the shipments were made by sea, the FBI will have to get involved. Is that why you want to have Trickten involved, Jacob? I think it's a good move to give him all the information we have. The LAPD can make the necessary arrests and then cooperate with the Feds when they ask for it. I guess Mr. Profacini will be smiling since none of this actually touches his organization. Padilla is as good as dead considering he'll never get out of jail alive. With the elimination of five of his boys the other night it will definitely place a damper on his power, if he has any left that is," said the police detective.

"Have to agree with you on that one, Bill. From now on, I have the feeling Mr. Padilla will not have the power to order an ice cream cone. The sad part is that we are never rid of these cockroaches. One dies, two new ones pop up. It's a real vicious circle we have to deal with day in, day out. At least we should have some quiet time ahead of us, don't you think so, Lieutenant?"

Bill Jones said, "Tell me, Jacob, what is the reason you invited me to lunch in the high society district? It was not to talk about Padilla, Paluka or Edwards, was it now?"

"Yes it was," said the gumshoe. "Don't you find our conversations invigorating? You and I are solving the problems for the people of southern California and possibly elsewhere too. On a more serious note, I think I have found the solution to the murder of Louis Billings, former bookie, pimp, arms dealer and many other indescribable roles. So far, this is for your ears only. I could be way off base and would not want the world to know. In any case, should I be right, I still would not want the world to know it came from me. This is why, before I tell you my well-thought-out plan, I want your word that you and the LAPD, of course, will take credit for it. Do we have an agreement, Mr. Bill, Lieutenant Jones?" Jacob asked.

"I don't know what you have in mind, Jacob, but I give you my word, as a friend, your name will never be mentioned in the final report. It would be embarrassing to me and the department if the public was to find out a private eye with no big budget solved one of the biggest criminal investigations on drug trafficking, bookmaking, etc, the LAPD ever had. Now quit stalling and tell me what you have found that no one else could," the lieutenant concluded.

CHAPTER TWENTY-FIVE...

Jacob had completed his fourteen-page report on Earl Edwards. It was only two days ago when Leon Edwards had sat across from him, pouring out his soul to a total stranger. The private eye had felt compassion for the father of a son who had brought him nothing but grief from the time he was a young teenager.

This weekend was the wedding of his Marine friend Alexander Fitzsimmons. He found out during a conversation at a stag party for Alex that they were in need of a washer and dryer. Jacob had ordered the units to be delivered one week before the wedding. This way he would not have to carry anything else but flowers, because Lorraine insisted on bringing them to the reception. It's always a nice touch she had said and women like flowers at any time.

His meeting with the FBI and his friend Lieutenant Jones had gone very well. Trickten was in agreement about seizing the garment shipments coming in from the East coast. Jacob thought that by doing so it would give everyone a chance to coordinate their actions and arrest a number of people almost simultaneously. This would be great publicity for the FBI and the LAPD. Narcotics were beginning to be a major problem all over southern California. For once, the law enforcement agencies would appear to have the upper hand on the drug traffickers. He had not told the decisive factor to anyone yet. Will they be surprise when they find out how Jacob solved the Louis Billings murder case? At the moment, everyone knows Tony Padilla's men had executed it. That part was not difficult, but Padilla had not ordered the demise of a guy who helped him rake in millions of dollars month in, month out in either drug trafficking or arms dealing. His obsession about finding out why the body had been dumped in his office led him to the one who ordered the hit. He even found out that $30,000 had been paid for the hit. His mental exercises ended when the sound of the ringing telephone brought him back to reality.

"Schreiber here," he said in his usual straightforward tone.

"Jacob, this is Jack Fundalee, the DA. I need to have a talk with you about some upcoming events Lieutenant Jones has briefed me on. When is it convenient for you?" he politely asked.

Jacob could not believe how mellow the DA was for a change. He thought quickly to put one over on this guy once and for all. "Why don't you be my guest at the Wilshire Country Club for lunch either today or tomorrow? I'll leave that up to you," Jacob concluded with a smile in his tone.

"I didn't know you were a member of the Wilshire upper-class gang, Jacob. One would never guess that a private investigator would hang around such prestigious grounds. On the other hand, it is the right place to pick up corporate clients. Today will be fine. Is 1 o'clock okay with you, Mr. Schreiber?" Fundalee added with a touch of sarcasm in his voice.

"Sure, Mr. District Attorney," Jacob said. "See you at one." After he hung up Jacob could not stop having a good laugh. His fast thinking had made him take advantage of the situation and catch the DA off-guard. Now he was sure that everyone in City Hall would know about Jacob Schreiber being a member of the very prestigious Wilshire Country Club. Could it be that from now on the DA's office would look upon Jacob Schreiber, private investigator, as a special person? *Wow*, he said to himself, *and I don't have to run for office.* He was sure his friend Lieutenant Jones would get a chuckle out of this. How can he not when you have to deal with a stiff upper lip like Jack Fundalee on a daily basis? On his way out, he decided to stop by the bank for some cash. As he was leaving the teller's counter, he saw the bank manager coming in his direction.

"Good morning, Mr. Schreiber," the manager said. "Would you have a moment to spare, I'd like to have a word with you, if I may."

"Certainly," Jacob said, as he followed the man toward his office.

The bank executive explained to him there had been a small error made in the deposit his secretary brought in the other day. It happened to be a new clerk and she had posted $500,000 dollars

THE BOOKIE

instead of $50,000. They found the error almost immediately and corrected it.

"Oh, yes I remember Anne telling me that on the way back from the bank she noticed the amount the teller had written in. She said she had immediately returned to the teller and had it corrected. Not a problem, sir, as long as we did not spend it all. Now that would have upset you," Jacob said with a grin on his face.

The bank manager was a bit embarrassed by the situation and he just wanted to reassure Jacob of the services they had and how they considered him a privileged customer. Anytime he would be in need of any of the services offered by his bank, he should not hesitate and ask for him immediately.

Why did they not use this kind of approach with me when I first started my business? He knew why. His deposits had more than quadrupled in the last six months. That was why.

He arrived at the country club some twenty minutes early. He needed to chat with the Maître D' before the DA arrived. This guy was his best source of information when he needed to know something about rich people. A hundred-dollar tip always helps loosen the tongue.

"I see you found the place without too much of a problem, Jack. Could I offer you an apéritif before we order lunch?" Jacob politely asked.

"You know, Jacob, I must admit this is my first time here. It's as nice as people have described. Whatever you have, I'll have," the District Attorney said.

"I know you have a political campaign coming up soon, so I've decided to make a contribution to help you get re-elected. Here's a check for $5,000 dollars. I added a three-month membership to this club in your name," Jacob said with a smile, looking at his guest who had a look of surprise on his face. "You'll be able to take the Mayor and even the Governor for lunch during that time. Hope you don't think I'm too forward, Jack. Just want to make sure you have the right tools to stay in office. That's what you want, isn't it?"

"Thank you very much, Jacob. I certainly appreciate what you have just done. My office also likes the open attitude you take when we have to deal with unpleasant business. Your cooperation with the DA's office and the LAPD tells us you are a solid citizen. Most other private investigators have a hard time with honesty. I wonder if they deal with their clients in the same manner."

"Jack, as you know, my father was a member of the LAPD and was killed on duty. He was a straight shooter who believed in the truth. He taught me to be as honest with others as I am with myself. I try to follow his example. I wanted you to have these contributions before my second guest arrives. I did not want you to feel pressured. Here he is now. Come have a seat, Lieutenant, I was just about to order us a pre-lunch drink," Jacob said.

"I'm sure amazed at how you move things, Jacob. I could use a guy like you in my campaign," said the District Attorney.

Jacob answered, "Not a chance, Jack. I like my freedom, it allows me to find and do things I could not normally do under a political umbrella. You both know I'm a stickler for law enforcement. First because of my father and then the Marines, under the best commander a recruit could have."

"That commander he's talking about, Jack, was my brother. Remember, you were at the funeral," Bill Jones said.

Jacob said, "I managed to get you both here knowing that you Jack wanted to talk to me about the garment case I am handling for Watts Enterprises. And you Bill to talk about Earl Edwards and his dealings with the garment designers in Los Angeles and New York. I'm willing to talk about all of it, but only after we have lunch and then after I tell you both who had Louis Billings killed and why."

Both men looked stunned, this private eye was going out of his way to place his number one obsession on the table.

Jack said, "I thought the lieutenant here told me that Tony Padilla had Louis Billings murdered. Am I missing something here, gentlemen?"

Jones said, "That's exactly what I had said and what the FBI also believed happened. Our friend here seems to have a different opinion and from what I hear him say, he has proof."

THE BOOKIE

Jacob said, "It is not that complicated once you look at all the different possibilities. What we have done, I mean all of us including me, is assume that Mr. Padilla, because of who he is, was the guilty party. Don't get me wrong, Tony Padilla is guilty of many murders for which he was never prosecuted because he was never caught. It was the beginning of the end for him when Jack Paluka decided to dump Louis' body in my office. For them, it was convenient and easy. They didn't realize the mistake they had made by violating the privacy of my office. Because Louis' wife Helen had been my client, it made it easy for me to have access at Billings' personal possessions. That's when I got lucky and discovered all the hidden assets, notebooks and whatever other paper trail Louis 'The Snake,' in his wisdom, had left behind. Any questions at this point?" Jacob asked.

They both said, "No, not right now. Let's hear the end of it, if there is one."

"Yes there is an end, and I'm getting closer to it. To make you both believe my scenario and the proof I'm going to lay out, I have to unfold the story as I see it. Louis Billings was known on the streets of Los Angeles as a bookie. To some special clients, he was also a pimp, a drug pusher and a loan shark. Only less than a handful of people knew about the military weapon deals with Eastern European and African countries. What I'm going to emphasize here is the pimping aspect. Louis dealt with prostitutes, females and males, the majority of them with a drug habit. He knew it was becoming more difficult for Padilla's group to move drugs across the nation so he engineered a whole new concept to move cocaine and heroin. His new concept, though, required different contacts that were willing to accept the risk. Louis had chosen the garment industry because of one contact he once had. Yes, one contact by the name of Earl Edwards, who one day approached Louis for drugs. Being what he was, The Snake immediately saw this young man as his essential player. He tested him a couple of times and found out it would be easy to deal with him, no matter how much cocaine he wanted. Louis set up an office to operate his new service from. He made the bookings for Earl to fulfill, always with rich men at first, who were known homosexuals, and with designers. Then he moved on to manufacturers of garments for both women and men. There he hit the jackpot. Most of these men had kinky habits and it became easy to hook them up with Earl. Then the extortion and fear game began. At first it was not very successful, so he had to set an example by having a Boston designer murdered in his own workshop. The word got around and the cooperation gate was wide open. Cocaine was being moved in shoe boxes, women's handbags, you name it, Louis used it. Padilla was quite proud of Louis for setting up this operation. It allowed the Mafia to move tons of drugs in a very short time." Jacob paused for a moment and ordered coffee for everyone.

"Now to conclude my story, I have here a copy of two medical reports for you to read. The first one is from a doctor in Dallas, Texas, which shows he treated Earl Edwards for two venereal diseases. The second one is from a doctor in Beverly Hills who treated Bill Watts, the designer, for a venereal disease. Louis Billings introduced Earl Edwards to Bill Watts. Bill Watts paid for the hit on Louis. He was upset at being infected by someone Billings had introduced to him. I found this letter in Louis' briefcase. It is written by Watts on his own stationery. If you take him in for questioning, Lieutenant, with this evidence you're sure to get a confession," Jacob proudly concluded.

Both the DA and the Lieutenant stared at him in disbelief.